THE SQUIRM FILES

includes

SQUIRM

STRUM

THE WELL-HUNG GUN

by

CARI SILVERWOOD

To join my mailing list and receive notice of future releases:

http://www.carisilverwood.net/about-me.html

If you'd like to discuss the Squirm Files or other books by Cari Silverwood with a group of other readers, you're welcome to join this group on facebook: https://www.facebook.com/groups/864034900283067/

CONTENTS

ACKNOWLEDGMENTS

Disclaimer

This book contains descriptions of BDSM and tentacle-themed sexual practices but this is a work of fiction and as such should not be used in any way as a guide. The author will not be responsible for any loss, harm, injury or death resulting from use of the information contained within. Especially if you stick anything up your nose.

SQUIRM

A parody of everything great and weird in erotic romance that could be stuffed into one book without it exploding.

For some girls, one tentacle isn't enough.

Having a bad day isn't good but when Virginia Chaste has a bad day, she gets felt up by a tentacle monster. If it simply has to happen, let it at least be a billionaire and a hot biker.

Virginity isn't all it's cracked up to be and her search for the Holy Grail of Erotic Romance, the ten inch purple-headed schlong, may have finally borne fruit.

Yeehaw! Playing hide the tentacle has never been so much fun.

CHAPTER 1

Virginia swept back her long, blonde hair and smiled as enticingly as she could at the man on the other side of the chain mesh gate. Her little, black dress was fine but the six inch, red stilettos were going to kill her any second. He grinned back, anchoring his fingers high in the mesh, leaning on the gate, and exuding eau de biker. The muscle of his flexed and tattooed bicep shone under the florescent light.

"C'mon in. We don't bite much. Name's Jace."

She breathed in again, swooned, then swiftly recovered and slipped past Jace into the garage.

Eau de Biker. *Mmm.* Oil, leather, and beer smells always did it to her. Her panties had wet through in an instant.

But, she had a job to do.

The garage was dark, dingy and filled with testosterone-hyped, tatted-up bikers. They roamed across the concrete floor checking out the chromed bikes like a pack of thirsty, hungry snakes let loose on a Sunday picnic of virginal, squeaky mice.

She shook her head, knowing she'd imagined that with way too many adjectives. Sometimes her imagination went a little ga ga.

Past the knowledge that she was here to look for Cyndie, she wondered, ever so hopefully, if among these men she would find her holy grail – what she'd been saving herself for from the day she opened the pages of her first romance novel – the man with the ten inch purple-headed schlong.

Fabio with his flowing locks could take a hike.

"Whatcha want, beautiful?" Jace didn't move from his gate

8

propping position and the space on the floor left over from men, machines, and crates was barely wide enough for both of them. She craned her head back.

Tallish. Check. Built like a bull. Check. Were there tingles in her downstairs department? *Mmhmm. Check.* Her pearly gates had gone into override and the doors were ready to burst open.

His crotch? Over the years she'd developed a package bulge versus true schlong-length chart. The holes she'd had to drill in men's toilet doors... But at least her carpentry skills were maxed out and she could now construct a bookshelf all by herself. Should she look?

Tongue on lip, her gaze strayed down his sculpted body over the oil stains on his T-shirt, past the splatters from spilled pizza, lower. *Chest. Hips.* She licked her lips but braked, restraining herself from venturing further. She didn't want to seem too eager.

The gleam in his eyes said he'd noticed.

"I'm looking for my friend, Cyndie."

"Don't know the name. She's probably not here." He leaned in even closer until she could count the bristles on his poorly shaven chin. "But you're pretty. You can stay. Turn around and spread your legs so I can fuck you up against the wire. I'll get my cock in you so deep it'll need a directory to find its way out."

"That sounds...dangerous."

"I am," he rumbled sexily, like a waterfall that's had a dam collapse upstream and is about to flood and destroy the village of peasants further downstream...many of whom are poor and in desperate need of medical attention.

She inhaled his delicious male scent again. "Why do you smell so good?"

"This." He held up a small bottle. *Eau de biker.*

"Fuck. I knew it," she whispered. "What's the pay?"

"For wall fucking?"

"Yes."

"Zero. But you get to be mine and we can have ten kids and though I may die early from multiple gunshot wounds we'll never regret a single moment of our existence."

"I see. Tempting." She sucked on her lip, thinking. *Cut to the chase.* "Schlong size?"

His brows shot up. "Oh baby. Nine inches."

An inch short. Her heart sank and she sighed sadly. "I'm sorry,

Jace. Ask me again tomorrow."

The garage door wound up, creaking like an armored tank in the throes of having a baby tank by painful cesarean section. Jace ignored it. The burst of light through the door, from glaring headlights, made most of the men rise to their feet.

"Cyndie left this." Virginia handed over the card.

Jace frowned as he read the back of the business card. He flipped it to read the front where a logo with a red octopus gripping a ship's wheel was embossed on the luxurious cream.

"Says she went to the club house of the Sea Wolves. Not us. You got the wrong place, Snookums."

Snookums? "I thought you were the Sea Wolves?"

"Nope."

Car doors slammed and two men walked in, ducking under the mostly open door, shoving it up higher. Though both were tall, one was a head higher than the other, and wider too. His boots were... They were... Virginia peered. The concrete seemed to sink around the boots.

Light streamed in past them like it had a contract to announce the arrival of a pair of avenging archangels. Except they didn't have wings and one of them, the biggest one, looked as if he'd fallen off the back of a truck, face first. And then someone had stapled a new wire-brush hairstyle on his scalp. If they were archangels, Heaven needed a new personnel department.

"Who the fuck are you?" someone yelled over the sound of the truck engine. "Rude fuckers. Ever heard of knocking?"

"I am Karl Thulhu," the first, shorter one, drawled in bass mode, his voice assertive yet relaxed. "This is my helper, Dangerous Bob."

Though he didn't in any way gesture at the big man beside him, she knew who he meant since Dangerous Bob had growled, low and menacing, and not at all like he meant to sell cookies or break into song about daisies or tulips...or anything to do with being happy.

"Dangerous Bob?" someone jeered.

"You don't want to know. He tones it down so he can fit into polite society." Karl smiled.

With the brightness of the light, she couldn't see his eyes but the smile was awesomely nasty. His voice was suave and educated but with a hard edge – he'd cut you without hesitation with an antique silver knife.

Dangerous Bob growled again, patently agreeing.

"So. You're such nice people. I can see that. Now that we've introduced ourselves, it's your turn."

The bikers' hands tightened on the baseball bats and wrenches they clutched. A few drew knives.

"Twats." Jace chuckled, drawing Virginia's attention back to him. "You said Sea Wolves. You see any ocean round here? A motor cycle club called that?"

"Not interested in playing nice? Listen, Furry Wolves!" Karl Thulhu said, just loud enough to be heard over the idling engine. "You've stolen my merchandise! And if there's one thing you don't do, it's steal from me."

"You're the Furry Wolves?" Virginia couldn't help sniggering.

Jace bent and picked a tire lever off the floor, the metal scraping on the concrete. Then he rose to stare at the two men. "You better go, girl. Things are about to get fucked up. Ain't no one claims off the Wolves."

A fight was going down.

"You want some?" A Furry Wolf member challenged, tapping a piece of lead pipe in his hand.

"Some what?" Karl Thulhu asked.

The entire garage full of Furry Wolves surged toward him and Dangerous Bob.

CHAPTER 2

The headlights went out, the engine stopped, then the garage lights also died. Blackness reigned. Screams and thuds proliferated. Feet scuffled. Metal clanged.

Quiet, except for the ticking of a cooling engine. Moans. Then lightning flashed from a storm that hadn't been in the vicinity a moment before. In the eerie and very convenient light, she caught a glimpse of a tableau – a monstrous beast towered above the bodies of the bikers, flailing at them with its terrible long arm things. The room darkened again.

What was the name of those long arm thingies?

Started with T.

Virginia tsked. Nope, she couldn't remember.

After a few more thuds and cracks that echoed off the concrete, the moaning ceased.

Dark. Quiet. It was black as midnight at the bottom of a very black hole in the ground, after someone has filled it in. Heavy, slapping footsteps came her way. Was a scuba diver loose in here?

"Jace?" she ventured. "Where are you? Are you alri –"

Something firm, moist, and oddly squishy grabbed her around the waist and flung her up against the metal gate. While she wriggled and screamed another squishy blunt something prodded at her cheek, slapped her lightly, then paused a moment. She heard distant sniffing and couldn't help shuddering.

Escape! But she was stuck there, feet dangling above the concrete, her arms pinned to her sides.

"Let me go?" she squeaked out.

Someone went *hmm*. The odd fleshy something slid down her body, probing her as it went. Over breast, into her belly button, drawing a teeny tiny circle...why had she worn such a thin dress? Then it went down her belly, poking at her hips before slithering around her back above the curve of her butt to *squeeze* her whole body once, then it retraced its path to her front. Onward, downward, on its sliding, slipping trail. Next, it found her mons. She held her breath as the long thing cruised between her legs and forced her to part them.

No panties! Why had she forgotten to put them on today? It wasn't as if she'd been *told* not to. Considering she'd planned to visit a biker club house, she should have put some on. Now, horror of horrors, this unknown thing that reminded her of a tentacle, but of course it *wasn't* one, it was about to violate her.

"Stop! Please?"

No answer.

Suddenly, very suddenly, with all the suddenness of a man eyeing a nude sunbather having his eye poked out by an umbrella, the thing probed her entrance. It shifted aside her lips. It was so gentle yet horribly disturbing, in a *hot*, nice way. Virginia gasped and clamped her legs onto the thing that also pressed upon her clit, but not because she wanted it to remain there, of course. That would be dirty. She felt herself dampen.

The thing quivered.

Oh my. She stared, eyes wide, out into the room. That was new.

It quivered again.

Was this what vibrators did?

Her thoughts derailed, and went chugging off on a whole amazing train track she hadn't known existed. *Toot toot.*

Quiver. Then it slid, back and forth, in her wetness.

Fuck, fuck, fuck. Ohhh crap. She was never blinking again. Her throat tightened. Her groin grew heavy and pulsed with every heartbeat. Her nipples joined in, poking out into the dress. She'd forgotten her bra too. How forgetful.

If she didn't stop this quivering from continuing, she was certain the world would do something weird.

What and who was this creature, doing this horrible wriggling on top of her clit? Mouth open, she squirmed again, and could hear them breathing before her, hard, rough, staccato. A little gurgly also maybe, but she wasn't dwelling on that part. *Shiver.*

Scream again, the little voice in her head whispered. *Time to scream. Scream?*

Go away! she whispered urgently back at her voice.

Fine! her internal voice replied. *If you want me again, I'll be sulking in the corner.*

She didn't care. The quivery, slidey thing was dabbling in her moisture. She was aroused, embarrassed, blushing hot.

"I'm a virgin!" she blurted, struggling against the implacable hold around her waist, but it still held her arms to her sides.

She was keeping herself for that ten inch schlong, remember? Remember! Inspiration arrived. "I recently had a bear trap installed...in my inside womanly parts."

The thing stopped probing her.

A strange questioning grunt encouraged her to go on.

"Yes. I did. And there's big metal teeth too. Anything that goes in me gets chomped on."

The reply sounded like a man pretending to be a puzzled dog.

"It's true."

She was let down from the wall, released.

Her lie had worked. *Damn.*

As she pressed back into the gate, shaking a little, with the metal mesh springing under her palms, there were crackling noises before her.

The lights flickered on.

Exasperated and horny, Virginia scowled and thought of the author, all snug at her desk. She recalled the previous pages, with their overflowery similes and the almost deflowering by a tentacle thingummy of an innocent maiden, her, Virginia Chaste, and she sighed. Perhaps today was not the best day to be in an erotic story.

CHAPTER 3

Karl Thulhu stood before her, his head tilted to the side. "Hello."
"Um." She made herself step away from the gate, terribly aware that only moments before she'd been imminently about to do something unusual – something that was because a creature had been probing her pussy lips.

She'd been about to *come*, she realized. Surreal. Perhaps Jace had slipped her a drug and she hadn't noticed? Beneath the dress, her thighs were slippery.

"Hello," she said, and her gaze lowered until she encountered Jace lying a few feet away to the left. He was snoring. As were all the many men lying on the garage floor. Only her, Karl, and Dangerous Bob were standing. And she was shaking. There were odd pinkish circles all over Jace's neck and arms.

They reminded her of something a big suction cup would leave on skin, like perhaps from a...

Puzzled, she cast her gaze about the garage, wondering nervously if there was a violent plumber running amok with one of those pipe unblocking plungers. There was no one, only Karl Thulhu, with Dangerous Bob a few feet behind him, and a lot of knocked-out bikers with pink blotchy circles on them.

"What's happened to them?"

"I think Dangerous Bob may have hit them a little," Karl replied. Some knuckle cracking followed from his henchman.

"You'd better not have hurt them permanently!" She scowled. "I liked that one. Jace."

"He'll be perfectly okay when he wakes up." Karl studied her, as if bemused by her concern. His navy T-shirt, jeans and black leather jacket contrasted with his posh accent, and his black boots looked as if a butler had shone them. But that, or the breadth of his shoulders, did not keep her attention.

The crotch bulge was momentous. *Ten plus!* screamed her early warning schlong alert.

No. Impossible. He might be a sock stuffer. She rolled her tongue back in and shook her head. "So all those blows to their skulls won't cause any neurological problems like concussion, bruising of the brain, blood clots, residual memory loss, or seizures in years to come?"

As if bewildered, he scrubbed his hand through his short blond locks. Virginia admired the orange streaks running across his hair. That same orange she'd seen on the monster when lightning had flashed into the room, searing her mind with that incredible scene of violence and long arm thingies.

What gorgeous hair.

"Absolutely not. They'll wake up with mild headaches." He smiled at her while Dangerous Bob sidled away to use a piece of four by two to pummel a biker who was up on his elbows. "Come. You have a dinner date with me at my mansion."

"I do?" Virginia frowned. "I'm sure it's not in my planner." He could be right, though. She'd already forgotten her panties, her bra, and what to call long arm thingies on monsters.

"Tentacles!" she blurted.

"What?" He flinched and looked taken aback and his brows creased as if some terrible thought had crossed his mind, such as murdering her on the spot.

"Nothing. I just remembered something. A word that might be important."

"Hmm." He cocked an amused eyebrow. "Tentacles? Yes. You could be right."

What a doofus she'd been. Now he'd wonder if she was an idiot. She scrambled for a way to redeem herself.

"Aren't you forgetting something too? You said they stole merchandise from you."

"Of course!" He turned. "Dangerous Bob. The crates. Bring in the rest of the Sea Wolves."

So these were the Sea Wolves? Now she had a good reason to stick close to this Karl.

At a whistle from Dangerous Bob, twenty or thirty hulking men ran in through the garage door and began carting away the crates.

"Oh my." She blinked. "Why didn't you ask these to help you in the fight?"

From one passing crate, he plucked a small multi-colored sculpture and brought it to her. "I like to keep my tenta– my hand in. Being a billionaire can make it too easy." His smile left his eyes and they seemed to darken as he let his gaze travel down her body. "Easy makes me want to do things the hard way."

Clearly he expected her to understand that. She nodded. "Uh huh." Weird man. "What is that?"

He hefted the sculpture and held it up for her to see. "A garden gnome. Ming dynasty."

She raised an eyebrow, lowered it, and raised it again. A gnome. Thoughts scrambled about the walls of her mind playing ball and catch me if you can. What in the world did he want with garden gnomes? A white powder was leaking from one cracked nostril. *Ah-hah.* She put her finger out and pressed it to the powder.

"Are all these crates full of gnomes?" Virginia put her powder-coated finger in her mouth and sucked.

"Yes. All of them. What was that on your finger?" He looked at the gnome's face. "Cracked?"

"Bolivian," she murmured. "Ninety percent pure. Barely cut at all." *Wow.*

If all these crates were packed with cocaine-filled gnomes this was worth squillions. No wonder the bikers had stolen them.

"Cracked," Karl Thulhu repeated. He tossed the gnome at the far back wall of the garage and it smashed, sending up a cloud of powder. "Damn."

What? "I thought." Her voice squeaked. "I thought you wanted these?"

"I know they're not worth much. It's a hobby of mine." He made tut tutting noises. "But once cracked they're not collectable."

Her mouth was stuck in an O of astonishment. Beyond Karl she saw Dangerous Bob grin and shrug as if to say, *what the fuck, I have no fucking idea.*

"Come." Karl held out his hand for her to take. "We have a small journey to make and you have to make a choice."

"I do?"

He gripped her hand tightly then strolled with her by his side out the garage door and into the night. "I overheard a conversation. Was it true that you are a virgin, and that you have a bear trap in your pussy that chomps on cocks?"

Oh my frickin god. She blushed so thoroughly her cheeks were probably on fire. "I umm..."

Something prompted her to be truthful. Probably the part of her that her aunt said should have been committed all those years ago after she ran across the football field naked except for a pair of pom poms and a tube of lube.

She sucked in a breath. "Yes. I am one. A virgin. But no, there is no bear trap. I made it up. I was sure a monster had hold of me." *And was violating my private parts.*

"Shh. It's fine. Don't be embarrassed. I like virgins. The bear trap seemed far-fetched but my brain doesn't do so well when I shift."

Shift. She checked Karl Thulhu out the corner of her eye. Had he moved house recently and what did that have to do with her being a virgin? She should just act intelligent, maybe?

"Lovely night out –" She halted. "What the hell is that?" An enormous black helicopter was parked in the street, with gun turrets and rockets slung beneath its stubby wing pods.

"AH-64D Apache Long Bow attack helicopter." Karl squeezed her hand. "I hate plot conundrums. Deciding how to beat up the Furry Wolves left me too many options – either show my own physical capabilities or show how obscenely rich I am. I decided to show my mean streak."

He let go of her hand, wrapped his arm about her waist, and dragged her to him until she had to lean back to avoid ending up face first in his jacket.

Startled, she let out a squeak.

The smile that spread across his face was almost demonic and she wondered if she should tell him in case he needed a makeover. No, being scared took precedence. Her heartbeat did a fast tango then fled to another country.

"I have one important question to ask you before I kiss you."

Kiss her? Her eyes had possibly bulged out of their sockets. Not good. "What?"

"Are you allergic to calamari?"

"Umm." She ran her tongue across her upper lip. "No? I think?"

"Good." Then he lowered his mouth to hers and kissed her so long and hard that by the time they were done she was panting, their tongues were tied in a knot that took them a minute to untangle, and her second almost-orgasm was ready to explode through her veins. She wanted to grind herself on that possibly ten inch plus long schlong, and scream, *take me*!

Also, the sun had arisen. One long-ass kiss.

"That was nice," she whispered.

"Yes. And now I know you're not allergic."

Hmm. This man was so curious. Garden gnomes and calamari allergies. Whatever next?

CHAPTER 4

Eye color, that was what was next, she realized, as he half drew and half towed her toward a herd of motor bikes. He had black eyes. Not black from being hit by Dangerous Bob's piece of four by two, but black irises like the yucky tasting jelly beans. Contact lenses, she decided.

Dangerous Bob was already astride his bike and he muttered something that sounded like, "Fuck. Fuckitty grumble fuck grrr." But in her head it came out as, *about time. Let's hit the road before the cops arrive.*

She blinked and he gave her a thumbs up.

Two girls appeared from nowhere and ran screaming at Dangerous Bob only to be left jogging in his dust as he took off.

"What was that?"

Karl appraised her. "He attracts them like flies. You've heard of catnip? Bob has girlnip. Whenever he swears women come running."

"Really?" Internally, she did a survey. No, no lady bits party. "Not me."

"You've got a rare immunity."

Karl picked her up around the waist and deposited her onto the back of the bike. Her bare wet pussy immediately slurped across then suctioned onto the leather. She dearly hoped he had some good leather cleaner. He sat in front of her, yelled, *hang on tight*, and started the bike. The three trillion whatever horsepower engine revved, like it was the beginning of a moon mission, the dawn sun glinted off the back of Karl's black jacket, and she frowned, thinking.

The whole flock or pack, or whatever the hell you called a collection of bikers, swerved and bumped over the sidewalk and onto the road then screamed forward, full throttle.

Elderly neighbors leaped out of the way and into the bushes, angrily shaking their crutches and wheelchairs.

Wow. Virginia raised her brow. Strong old people.

Wait on. The handlebars of the bike, the glimpse she'd had of them, had been of some immense sparkling. She edged up off the seat, feeling her twat reluctantly release the leather, and spied over his shoulder. *Yup. Good guess.*

"Are those diamonds on your bike, Karl?"

"Yes!" His word was torn away by the wind and the noise of the growling bikes. "I keep the attack helicopter on standby to guard from thieves."

Show off.

Diamond-encrusted bike handles!!!!!!!!!

Swoon time. Her ovaries, that really should know better, got up, chugged down a bottle of tequila, and did a naked tap dance.

She put her nose to his neck and inhaled. The smell of his sweaty neck had become as divine to her nostrils as the scent of a suitcase of money.

There was some weird sex appeal to a man who had diamond encrusted handlebars on his bike and a big nasty helicopter at his disposal to blow to smithereens any thief crazy enough to try stealing them. Maybe because it seemed as if he could protect her from all the bad things in life? He could buy his way out of anything, or into anything, like a trip to Paris for the weekend?

Love unlimited. Luxury unlimited. Yes. And if some bitch stole her place in the queue at Walmart, she could have her turned into duck food. *Scary vengeance unlimited.*

Her inner voice gathered courage and whined. *That's not very nice.*

Party pooper, she told it.

The bike accelerated. Woohoooo.

After tearing along the streets and highway for nearly an hour, though part of that time was spent buying gnomes at a local market, they arrived before a set of steel gates that were sculpted in the shape of waves. The gates swung open, the bike rolled in, and Virginia leaned out to study the hill the asphalt headed toward.

On top of the hill perched a dark, turreted castle that rose so high into the sky that clouds caressed the very top blood-red turret. She could barely make out the details of the flag up there. A red octopus clutching a wheel? The same design was on a patch on the back of Karl's jacket and, of course, on the business card Cyndie had left. Strange shapes like...like big spaghetti sprouted from the base of the castle and wound around and up the brickwork.

Perhaps Karl was Italian? That would explain his preference for red too. Like tomato sauce or something.

Seagulls and terns cruised above and she could hear waves washing onto shore. The ocean must be over the horizon.

As they began to climb the hill road, she stared in awe at the castle. "It's enormous."

"Too big!" he tossed back at her. "The damn cleaners always want overtime."

Though Karl was a commanding man, perhaps some small advice would help him.

"If you explain the circumstances, they might be kind enough to take less pay?"

He remained silent until they skidded to a halt, in a spray of gravel, beside the front double doors of the castle. The Apache attack helicopter thundered in and landed off to the side, scattering flowers, sucking a lone stupid seagull into its air intake, and swamping the sound of the arrival of the rest of the pack of...swarm of...skulk of, she'd heard that one somewhere, but whatever the hell you termed them, they had arrived too – the other Sea Wolves on their bikes.

"I tried explaining to the cleaners. I find throwing them off the roof works better."

"Mmm?"

The engine throbbed to a stop and still she hadn't worked that one out. What else sounded like throwing? *Maybe he meant hoe-ing. Stowing? Crap. No.*

Note: get hearing tested.

As he dismounted, she checked out the black leather gloves he wore with big red spots on the palms. Red, again. Black, red, sometimes gray. But orange and blond hair, at least that was different. The man needed some makeover team to kidnap him. And again with the creepy black and gray giant spaghetti curling over the red doors. A clap of thunder made her jump. Karl grinned and took her hand to help her off the bike. Some fool had a storm theme on loud speaker.

The rest of the bikers had lined up either side of the path to the doors, as if this was a rite of passage she had to make before she'd be allowed to enter. Some women sneaked out through the doors and wrapped their arms around a couple of the bikers. Karl introduced the bikers as he led her past. *Crank. Souleater.*

"Hi," Souleater growled. "This is Jennifer." The brown-haired woman peeked from under his arm and nodded, her smile packed with warmth and welcome. Souleater squeezed her in closer until she gasped. "Sorry, sweets."

Karl continued. "Heart Surgeon." My oh my, what a lot of scalpels that man possessed.

"Daisy." His sleeve of daisy tattoos commingled with ones of mermaids being toasted on a BBQ grill.

"Pretty." She faked approval. *Yup. Free ticket to the asylum there.*

Wanderer. Diamond Dick. Tiny. She had to squeeze past his enormous gut. After twenty or so men her head swam with names.

Their scents assailed her. Leather. *Mmm.* Beer. *Ohmigod.* Money. *Holy crap.*

She swayed.

They were all big and burly and in black or brown leather jackets. Any one of them could eat her for breakfast.

Or all of them. What a vision that conjured. Her naked and lying on her back on the table, wriggling. Them lowering their mouths, licking her toes, pulling apart her legs. Holding her down –

"This is Horse," Karl said.

Horse leered at her so obviously that she stopped. Another large man. A brown tail of hair pulled back by a leather strip.

She tried to but couldn't stop herself asking. "Why are you called Horse?"

"Why do you think, Honey?" He quirked an eyebrow, waggled them both and did a little groin thrust in her direction.

Leisurely, she roamed her gaze down him, *down, downnnn*, yes further. *Crap the man was big. Down. Found it. Hmm.*

She looked some more, sucked in her cheek. Small crotch bulge. She did the arithmetic.

Bulge volume P minus R thickness of cloth. Square root of I unrolled length of schlong and add C wanking time. Answer equals K.

Double *hmm*. *No. Do not.* But her many years of study of a thousand male appendages through a thousand drilled toilet doors meant she owed it to the world to reveal the stats.

"Let me guess. Because you're hung like one?"

"Yep. Want a trial run?"

She took a deep breath but the words spilled.

"The average stallion has a penis that when erect runs to about twenty-two inches long, yours is about seven and a half erect, a Shetland pony would beat you. Oops." She smiled, knowing she was going red. "Sorry."

"What the? How can you...how can you know that? Hey. That's. That's just plain wrong!"

Karl dragged her on by her arm. "He'll get over it."

"That's a lie! I can prove it!"

"Hey, Ponyman!" someone yelled, then they laughed. The sounds of a small fight with baseball bats and knuckle dusters, maybe the odd handgun, broke out behind her.

"Welcome to my dwelling and the club house of the Sea Wolves" Karl said as he pushed through the center of the doors. Beyond seemed only darkness. "We have a dinner date and you need to get ready." His lips stretched into a menacing smile that made both her ovaries faint and her inner voice get all choked up, for once.

"Okay," she squeaked.

Dangerous Bob was already inside, standing a few feet away at the forward edge of a vast stretch of black marble. A shaft of light illuminated him from above. The hairs on his head were indeed pieces of sticking up wire and tats of tiny black spiders ran across his scalp, filling in the color between the wires. His groin – for once her measurements availed her not at all. *Unreadable.*

The ceiling seemed to be up there, somewhere a long way away, as in a forever distance.

Dangerous Bob's string of profanity and murmured fucks and fuckitty's merged into the translation in her head, *Welcome, Virginia. I hope you know you won't be leaving here a virgin.*

Oh myyy.

Three screaming girls ran in and clutched at him. He patted them all then pulled one up until she jumped and clasped his waist with her legs, then he kissed her.

Karl chuckled. He tucked Virginia into his side and bit her neck, then he turned her so her back was spooned against his body, trapping her arms under his. At the feel of his hard length pressing into her, heat ran through her body like an Olympic torch carrier being chased by a pack of wild rabid dogs.

Her ovaries fainted again. Cheapshit ovaries. When she shivered and clutched at his arm so as not to fall, he laughed.

"That's Amber, Dangerous Bob's nemesis. She's the one who gave him a Kool-Aid hand job, turned his dick blue, and made it fall off. He has an artificial battery powered replacement. That's why we call him Bob – B. O. B. He vowed never to let her return to the land of reality again."

Reality land? Wait. The man had no schlong? Damn. This place was whacky. She so needed to watch her step. Things could go wrong. Like, what the hell, no schlong?

And what was a BOB?

"You're beautiful," Karl said, murmuring hotly in her ear and kissing her here, there, and anywhere that had a vague link to an erogenous zone. Something as thick as his arm slid across her stomach, below where his arms already held her, and ventured lazily southward. She tensed.

What. Was. That? Had a snake wandered in?

"Snake! Python! Or maybe some of that spaghetti stuff has gotten loose?"

Virginia tried to look but his grip firmed and she could only see his arms. When she struggled and went to speak, he shushed her, and rocked her side to side, growling a little.

A man growling in her ear was all fine but the rocking was freaking her out. Plus her arms were maybe going blue from his grip.

"Snake?" she repeated. "Feral spaghetti?"

"Neither, Virginia, it is I. You're mine from now on and you will never ever leave here again."

Shit. Oh shit, shit. In an emergency, the part of her brain that she normally devoted to her Quest for the Ten inch Purple-headed Schlong would drag itself out of the gutter and come help her think.

Think!

"Wait." She strained her forearm into view and held up a finger. "You said that I needed to make a choice. So therefore I choose to leave." It would devastate her to have to leave behind a possible ten plus incher but sacrifices were needed.

"You made your choice when you got on my bike with me."

A small twang of terror joined the twinge of fear she'd already cultivated.

She scrambled for another excuse. "And I have nothing to wear to dinner?"

"Pfft. Who said you needed clothes."

"Me?" she squeaked. Her heartbeat was thumping away like crazy in her chest. Which was a relief – if it'd been anywhere else in her body she'd have really been in trouble. "Karl. Umm. I'm not the main course, am I?"

"No. Of course not, my gorgeous captive virgin. You are dessert."

Virginia scrambled for a witty comeback but nothing arrived in her mind apart from a whole bunch of high-pitched screams and one of those solo violin efforts where the same horrible note went on and on. *Eee! Eee! Eee!*

The tip of the snakelike thing, which somehow was also Karl, had gone even further southward. When it timidly lifted her dress and sneaked underneath to poke around at the juncture of her thighs, she recognized it. This was the same thing that had come close to violating her before. She jammed her thighs together. Not this time, baby. This dessert was off the menu.

Tentacle! That word again. She'd remember it now, considering the thing had been partway up her twat.

Without a genuine smart ass reply, she could only kick Karl in the shins as he slung her over his shoulder to drag her off to dinner.

"Mwhahahahahaaa!"

It was so cheesy, but he had to be trying to scare her with the laugh.

"Evil laughter? Really?" She kicked and wriggled again. "That's not a good look."

"What about this?"

With her facing backward, she had a prime view of the back of his jacket, which split and erupted in a flurry, revealing a nest of huge tentacles that swished and curled before her face. She screamed, just a little. One tentacle slid over her back to flip up her dress and whack her bare ass.

"Ow! Quit that! You're not even Italian, are you?"

He kept leisurely walking and began to climb some stairs. "I'm a demonic creature from an alternate evil dimension."

"You are?" She sucked on her lip then dodged a stray waving tentacle as it pried at her mouth and played with her teeth. "I think that rules out Italian. Though maybe not Canadian."

CHAPTER 5

The dining table was thick glass and perched on a black glass balcony that overlooked a long dining hall fifty feet below. The far side of the dining hall fell away to a rocky shore and small waves curled in from a dark sea. The rest of the Sea Wolves dined down there, tossing food now and then into the waves that slopped across their floor. Their women sat on their laps or beside them, laughing and being fondled and kissed.

Only Dangerous Bob and Amber had been up here, serving the food.

It all looked fun except when one of the bikers transformed into some walrus-cross-shark creature, with snappy, sharp teeth, and slipped into the sea.

Crap. She should have left Cyndie to her fate. Friendship was over rated, as were alive friends. Who would take over and be the Schlong Quester if she died?

The surface of the sea churned and blood welled outward, staining the water red.

"Ohmigod," she squeaked.

Karl sat opposite with his back to the hall but he turned to look. "Daisy likes his food au naturel."

Virginia shivered, but not simply from fear. Karl had made her dress in a skimpy lace top and skirt outfit that was ninety percent air and one percent cotton. A cobweb would be less revealing and already one perky nipple was being strangled by the lace hole it had poked itself into.

Cold. Brrr. She shivered again, untangled her nipple, then glowered at Karl.

He eyed her nipple. "Pretty. Soon I will take you down to my sacrifice room where all potential virgins are trialed."

The implications in that were mostly bad. Ah well, at least the lobster and caviar had been tasty. Wait. Suspicious, she checked the Sea Wolves. Where had those fish eggs come from? She had a sudden urge to spit.

"Sacrifice room?" With one finger, she made her fork spin in a slow circle on the table. "I don't suppose you'd consider modernizing? I've heard red rooms of pain are way more fun."

"Nope. I will give a way out however." He sat back and smiled, all dead eyed and dark of manner. "If you can leave this table without having an orgasm, I promise I will free you unharmed."

He was going to rig this, she just knew it. "Try me, Mister." She showed her teeth and took her knife and fork in her hands. "What's the next course? Calamari – battered and fried?"

His smile twitched and he leaned in. "More like covered in cream. Yours."

"Cream?" She frowned. "Is this anything to do with a BOB?"

"Naïve virgins are such fun. Let me show you."

The moist crackling, she recognized from that time in the dark at the Furry Wolves garage. His jacket moved oddly and the table bumped, shadows writhing her way. Looking down, she spotted a multitude of his tentacles squirming across to her under the table.

One fondled her thigh and sucked on her knee. She shuddered.

"Stop that!"

When she jabbed at it with knife and fork, she nearly speared her knee since the tentacle whipped out of the way. "Damn you!"

A frenzy of tentacles enveloped her, grabbing her wrists and pinning them, curling about her body until she was wrapped tightly into the chair.

"Can't breathe," she gasped, pretending.

Looking amused, Karl only narrowed his eyes, examining every inch of her, especially her chest. "Where oh where do I begin? All that luscious, unravaged female flesh."

She stifled a whimper.

Dangerous Bob and Amber arrived either side of her chair, bearing more plates with some toffee and cream topped dessert.

"We won't be needing that," Karl murmured, resting his elbows on the table and folding his hands. "Virginia is dessert, though I think she'd forgotten. You're free to do what you wish, Dangerous Bob."

"Fuckitty fuck grr." The translation arrived. *Thank you, sir.*

Dangerous Bob grabbed Amber, stripped her dress from her in one motion and thrust her against the waist-high balcony glass. His hand went to his groin. The rrr sound was not from pants unzipping, she realized, shocked. A starter motor? The next noise reminded her of an outboard motor from a boat. Amber wriggled her butt at him then groaned as he slowly penetrated her with a big vibrating florescent green dick.

"Oh my!" She averted her eyes from their public display and remembered with a jolt that she too was on display.

Tentacles arrived between her legs, some slithering up to her breasts to tease both her nipples and then fasten onto them and suck. The subtle yet strong suction made her toes curl and her pussy swell to life and moisten. Though she wriggled her wrists and legs, everywhere was fastened down. Her eyes stayed wide open as heat surged, seemingly connecting her nipples and pussy in one ecstatic symphony of throbbiness.

"Karl," she pleaded. "No. This isn't –"

"Isn't what? Decent? Polite? No, it's not. Nothing I do with virgins ever is. I plan to explore every inch of you at leisure, but first I need to do as I said I would, I need to make you come."

"Never!" She shut her eyes to rustle up some resistance despite the never-ending *suck, suck,* and *suck* on her breasts.

"Never? You intrigue me. You have such knowledge of men's cocks and yet I sense a lack of knowledge about your own anatomy. To not know what a BOB is..."

"What." She cleared her throat. Ignore that feather-light touch on her thigh, the trickle of moisture from her pussy, and the brush across her clit. "What's a BOB?"

"A battery operated boyfriend. A vibrator used by women to bring themselves pleasure. Like this."

The tiny tentacle tip that had been lurking in the vicinity of her clit fastened itself over the top and began to suck in time with the ones at her breasts. If lust could have a solid presence, it was flowing through her now like a river of hot creaminess, all sticky, and sucky, and *nice.*

Like a Devonshire tea and scones but way better. Her mouth parted. *Mmm.*

"A simple feeling, I'm sure, but females of your species seem to like it."

She could feel her pussy opening a little more, moisture coming from her, dribbling down her skin, and wetting the chair.

The strangled noise she made was her attempt to say, *no*. Her eyelids fluttered halfway down and she twitched, and she found herself pushing her pelvis up from the chair to get more of that exquisite feeling.

"But that is nothing. This is what a vibe does."

The sucker over her clit sprang into action and down there her clit was grasped and quivered upon, as relentless as a washing machine set on the 1000 rpm spin cycle.

"*Ohmigod!*" Her eyelids slammed shut and she groaned, possessed by an impending sense of an oncoming unknown *something* that was surely going...to...be...*fucking...damn... Stop, stop, stop.*

Oh hell.

Go!

Her muscles locked and she exploded, writhing and gasping, trying in vain to gather enough oxygen to breathe properly while still coming. The tentacles held her in place or she'd have surely leaped into the air. The suckers pulled at her, drawing her flesh against them, coaxing, fluttering. A last scream took her.

When she ceased shuddering and dared to look up at Karl, she saw a smirk on his face that she'd have dearly loved to wipe off with a flamethrower, if only she wasn't so exhausted.

After some minutes, when she was sure she hadn't died of a heart attack and could hear, breathe, and see the world properly again, she noticed the loud motor noises had stopped. Dangerous Bob and Amber sat cuddling on a padded chair off to the side. The green thing that had replaced his schlong was motoring along quietly, purring.

Karl rose to his feet and the tentacles slipped away from her. Only one remained to caress her cheek as he walked around the table. He squatted beside her chair and took her limp hand, kissing it. "You were beautiful, Virginia. I assume that was your first?"

She glowered weakly. Smug bastard. Nowhere on her body had any reserve strength, so she stuck her tongue out at him.

His gaze fastened onto it. "You are giving me such ideas. Your mouth. Your lovely tongue. Your ass. I'm spoilt for places to play with and explore. And they're all virgin territory, aren't they, sweet delicious Virginia? It's time to visit my sacrifice room."

Her eyes sprang wide. "Wait," she begged huskily. "Don't I need an appointment? I'm free next Tuesday at two pm. Besides exploring needs preparation doesn't it? Plans. Lists of stuff for the journey. Torches, energy drinks, sherpas, pack mules..."

"Kinky, but I don't think you can fit all those up there."

"Don't bet on it. The things I've seen women in Thai bars insert up their hoohahs —"

"I'll keep that in mind." He winked. "But you won't delay the inevitable. Today is perfect. See." His gesture made her look toward the floor. The black surface cleared, becoming transparent in an instant.

Beneath them was a roiling, circling, whirlpool of redness, like a bloodshot eye watching them, beckoning them into its realm of horribleness.

"I'm pretty sure," she muttered, "I don't want to go down there. Hmm. Give me a second. Yep. I am sure." The man needed a new color to obsess over.

"But you're going anyway, and coming too. Whether you want to, or not."

She was beginning to think she should have brought a gun with her. A big one.

"Let's go." He picked her up and slung her over his shoulder again.

She couldn't help peeking at his back. *What the?* "Where'd they go? What'd you do with all your tentacles?" She shuddered.

"They sort of fold up. IKEA. Wait, I'm not allowed to mention brands like KFC or Target or Thulahoops. Not that those are at all relevant to undergoing bodily transformations or folding tentacles. Let's say I'm flexible."

"I think you just did mention them. And I've never heard of Thulahoops."

"Only in passing. No one will notice what I said all buried down deep in the story like this. Thulahoops are a soon to be enormously popular exercise device."

She nodded and shifted on his shoulder to get comfortable.

"Works for me."

"Good. Six dollars ninety-nine if you buy in the first week." He stumbled then cleared his throat. "What have you been eating?"

Virginia froze. "Are you saying I'm fat?"

"No. Of course not. Prepare to meet your tentacle, Virginia."

"Don't change the subject. You implied I was fat."

"Didn't."

"Did."

"Want a tentacle in your mouth?"

Damn. Unfair.

She shut up but glowered.

The silence on the way down the stairs was so awkward.

CHAPTER 6

By the time Karl had her where he wanted her, she was standing spread-eagled and stripped of all but a few shreds of lace. Her arms were drawn above and her legs spread wide for she was roped to two nearby, spaghetti infested-pillars. Sourly, she eyed the spag stuff again. If the spaghetti was meant to be a reasonable facsimile of tentacles writhing across the pillars, his decorator had failed.

The red whirling eye was hidden under a carpet. Thank god. It had been making her dizzy. Throwing up on Karl seemed so impolite, even if he did mean to violate her...she gulped, everywhere, putting those thick tentacles into her unsullied, unpenetrated places. She bit back a moan. Places that she'd often dreamed of inserting dildos and cucumbers into. Carrots, maybe too. Vegetables had so much potential.

Perfectly normal, she reminded herself. Besides, she'd never done it. Some of her friends boasted of putting rabbits up there, which seemed awfully uncomfortable, but she wasn't judging, and wasn't game to tell them that out loud.

The fur must be so itchy.

Along the wall, a few yards away to her left, stretched a console that would suit a mad scientist lair. Legs crossed at the ankle, Dangerous Bob lounged against it. He yawned, looking both bored and expectant. When he slowly perused her body, Virginia strained on the ropes to show him she wanted to be *free*, and not at all to make her boobs jiggle and stick out. He went a little red of face. After that, and adjusting his crotch, Bob uttered a single appreciative *fuck* then winked at her.

Useless man.

Karl prowled across the floor toward her, naked from the waist up, one tentacle in hand (*tentacle* not testicle, get your eyes checked) and a few others curling about him and trailing at his feet.

Imagine if that had been testicle, the mind boggles.

He was careful not to walk over where the eye was concealed.

His silence made her nervous and she nibbled on her lip. Being all nude in front of a man...testicle guy...monster person wasn't her thing. Especially when her pussy was aching.

Wait. That was *tentacle. Tentacle guy.*

He circled her while observing her every movement, her every jiggle and whimper, with that dark look on his face. His eyes were black as sin, his mouth still, his tentacle twitchy. Karl stopped before her.

Alas, whatever lurked in his pants was staying there for the moment.

She swallowed and met his eyes.

He smiled, leaned on one of the above ropes, and let his tentacle slither down it to stroke her neck.

"I've brought so many women down here and none have satisfied me."

Worried, she tested the ropes again and shifted her hips to the side, then bit her lip. Ow.

"What happens if you're not satisfied?"

"I throw them into the portal." He gestured at the rug. "They never return."

"Never? Oh dear. Did Cyndie go down there?" That must be it. She'd not seen her among the Sea Wolves and she'd vanished after coming here. "Where does it go to?"

"Cyndie? Who is that?" A second tentacle curled around her waist, down the curve of her bottom to play with her crevice near her nether hole.

"Hey! Watch where you're going there."

His smile turned devilish. "I know precisely where it is going. Cyndie, you said?"

She shut her eyes and shuddered. The tentacle probed her and, as small as the tip was, he could insert it without hurting her. Her toes curled as it forced itself a little further. "Stop. No. No more."

"Yes, more."

It wormed in further. Her opened eyes found his black ones riveted on her face, registering her gasps of surprise and pain.

"I remember Cyndie. She went into the portal. She was delicious but not good enough for me. Come to me my most gorgeous and most recent captive. I need to possess you, to take you, to make you *mine.*"

While the tentacle slowly withdrew, he kissed her forehead, her nose then her mouth. His lips played there, toying, teasing, arousing her, until she breathed in small pants and couldn't stop herself from grinding into him when he came close. He turned his head sideways and nipped her throat, sucking and biting on her while his tentacles and hands roved about her body, quietly stirring her.

Then he moved away and withdrew all of his bits that had been touching her. She stirred from the fog of desire, wiped the steam from her sex goggles, and metaphorically squeegeed away the drips. That really had been...*shiver*...exceptionally nice.

She would *not* think about what was trickling down the inside of her thighs.

Why, now that she wanted him, had he left her?

"Take off your pants," she pleaded. "I need to see you."

She needed to see more than the ridged stone-hard muscles of his chest and stomach, or the V of male hair leading the eye down to the waist where it vanished into his pants. As she studied him, she nibbled her lip again, careful not to bite the same place. It still hurt. She simply had to stop biting herself.

What she wanted to see tormented her. Though the rest of him on show wasn't bad either.

"You know, you're the first woman I haven't had to lure here. The first to get on my bike and come here of your own volition. Normally I have to attract them by other methods. Those."

She followed the line of his pointing finger to the glass display case. On each shelf was a plethora of ties.

"I have them all – fifty thousand of them. All of the grays – storm gray, pallid gray, dominant gray, and so on."

She frowned. "How?"

"How does it work? First, I intrigue the women by puzzling them with my many declarations of wanting to fuck them within an inch of their life against the nearest wall."

"Then you tie them up?"

"No. Then I lay a trail of ties all the way here and they follow it and fall into a pit just inside the gates." He shrugged. "It works."

"Ooo-kay." Not that suave. She screwed up her mouth, nodding and pretending not to be disappointed.

His step carried him closer. One tentacle whipped out and behind her, flicking across her butt, scoring it with fire.

"Owieee!" She danced as much as she could with the ropes holding her in place.

"You, Miss Virginia, will pay attention. Tell me why I didn't have to fool you. Why did you come here?"

Her gaze dropped to his package level. That tantalizing huge bulge was still there. Ten plus. *Oh myyy.* She let out a tiny groan. More wetness seeped from her. She was going to need emergency rehydration if this kept up.

Fire scorched her butt. She shrieked at the strike of the tentacle.

"Tell!"

"It was because I seek...I seek the ten inch schlong! I am the Quester of the Schlong." She sagged in the ropes, distraught at having to reveal her secret.

"Ahh. And you think I qualify?"

"Yes." She sobbed. "Yes. Are you my destiny?"

This time he circled her and approached from behind. He molded his body to hers, covered her bound wrists with his hands.

His words thrummed in, deep, imprinting themselves on her very deepest, deepest, deep bits.

"I believe I am your destiny. You are mine, as I am yours. We shall be one. So *one* that your air will be mine, your scent mine, your blood will fill my veins, your soul and my soul will entwine together forever. Everything about you, *mine*."

Wow. "Those little china animals on my mantelpiece?"

"Mine."

Teeny bit obsessed.

The revelation that this man, okay, this tentacle man, wanted her so desperately, almost exploded her heart from her body. Luckily, it did not. So messy that would be. Blood *everywhere. Ick.*

"Oh, Karl, I think I'm swooning. Though it's hard to tell with the ropes and all holding me upright. If we are so *one*, does that mean my mortgage is yours?"

"That...not so much."

"My period?"

"Absolutely not."

Darn. Worth a try.

"You know for a tentacle monster you're pretty tame. I mean here you've got me at your mercy and all you want to do is make me yours and sexually ravage me and give me orgasms."

She shrugged when all he did was rest his chin on her head and wriggle another tentacle across her butt between his body and hers.

"What else did you expect?"

"I don't know. Pain. Rending me limb from limb. Chewing on my bones. Driving me insane. Exploding my brain. Monster torture."

"Hmm. Most of that would mean a big extra cleaning bill. It's already huge. Plus I like tentacle sex. So. Instead I'll just brand your butt with *mine* before I ravage and violate you."

Sounded reasonable. She was nodding before the meaning hit her. "What? Wait!"

This time the fire lasted, eating into her butt right where that tentacle rested and gripped her, like tiny teeth filled with acid were gnawing on her. Which was possibly exactly what was happening.

She screamed and babbled but he held her tightly.

The fire ebbed, dying to a dull ache, though she would never forget that he'd branded her butt.

"What if," she gasped. "What if we change our minds? *Mine* doesn't turn into anything else. Like, what are the chances my next boyfriend would be called, umm..." She searched in her head. "Minetaur? Or, or –" A tentacle plastered itself across her lips. "Urk! Mmph!"

"Shh. There will be no others. It's me or it's the portal to the other dimension. Now, shut up, I have places on you to explore. Orgasms to bring forth."

She eye-rolled. *Bring forth?* What was it with the archaic dialogue all of a sudden? What was wrong with, *I want to make you come?*

*****

Warning.

The next part of the story is filled to the tippy top with tentacle sex. Well, there's some, a little tiny bit, enough that if you read onward you will be known henceforth by the label Tentacle Pervert. Read onward and when you have to fill in that spot on the insurance form where it asks if you've ever been arrested for chicken rustling or dabbled in things that would make all your aunties and granmas faint, you will have to tick yes.

You are on a slippery, depraved path. Tentacles, ahoy!

CHAPTER 7

You tentacle pervert, you.

*****

With the tentacle in her mouth, Virginia had no way of communicating all her worries, such as where had all those tentacles been before? Hygiene, man, hygiene. When another tentacle shimmied across her eyes, she couldn't even see what he was up to.

Had some of those been used to take out the garbage?

Or pick his nose?

One at least had been up her ass, and now, *oh fuck, oh fuck*, she could feel another seeking that same spot. She clenched her butt, indignant at the chuckle this elicited from Karl.

"Relax. My tentacles come with a special lube. You'll barely know they've gone in."

Oh sure, she wouldn't. Unless he could make her ass into a space and time bending tardis.

She attempted to communicate by gargling. "'an I ick wun up yer ass?"

"No."

The one in her ass did a wiggle, sliding an inch inward, and she did an indignant squeak.

"See, it went in. I have finesse. That's all you need for anal. Alpha tentacle finesse. Do that squeak again. I like your little noises of protest."

Next time she'd bring placards.

How many tentacles did he have? She'd not counted them all, but she figured he had some in reserve. *At least eight? It was logical wasn't it?*

Another tentacle writhed across her belly then went all the way around her body, twice, then headed down, down, over her mound. She sucked in a breath and held it. The thing wriggled atop her clit before it slid further, pushing aside her legs and cruising over her damp pussy lips, dead center along the seam, separating them.

It throbbed. Her clit, getting as wildly excited as a groupie humping the leg of a rock star, grew hotter, and bigger, and throbbed back.

Damn thing needed to learn who it belonged to.

Sensations. Sensory input focused down on what she could feel, could smell, could taste.

Nothing but blackness, and him behind her breathing on her neck, the ropes and tentacles gripping her, and the one suctioned onto her pussy. She swallowed, carefully, so as not to give that tentacle over her mouth any ideas.

Throb, throb.

Oh. Myyy goodness. That was *mmm*. Her eyes decided to roll up.

Despite the double tentacle grip on her head, Karl sank some fingers into her hair, and tilted her head back. Sightless, she wondered what he was doing, seeing. Her face, she supposed.

She strived to calm her breathing but couldn't help whimpering and panting as the sucking intensified, betraying her arousal.

"You're so fucking *wet*."

Huh? "'at's yer lube." Though some *was* her.

"Oh, yeah. Forgot." He licked her. "When I'm this close, this intimate with one of my victims... I mean virgins. Sorry, slip of the tongue. I find I can often hear their thoughts. Sometimes it's like smoke signals and vague. Or scribbles on the back of an envelope. You, Virginia, are giving me text messages with pictures."

"Ayy em?" she gurgled past the thing that was slowly invading her mouth, which was strangely and disturbingly erotic.

"You are." He panted in her ear. "You're fucking awesomely *tight* too."

This time she just thought it. *Because I'm a virgin, duh, and you're hung like an octopus cross elephant.*

His chuckle was ominous. "You know me so well." The tentacle in her ass shoved in a fraction more.

Oops. Her toes scrunched on the rug-covered floor. However did he clean off all the, *ahem*, fluids?

"Let's see. Yes, I cleaned all my tentacles. No, there was no nose picking. And it's twenty dollars an hour for the rug. Extortion. But I don't mind. Not when I have such a pretty victim."

"'irgin," she burbled.

"Virgin. Yes. I keep slipping, don't I?"

She would have agreed with that but a second tentacle had decided to mosey alongside the one separating her thighs and was right now, as of this second, feeling for her entrance with all the skill of a blind safe cracker.

Whoops. Not there. No. Not there either.

Eep. As it found the right place and squirmed into her, she wriggled her hips sideways. Slippery with her wetness, it sank further, one inch, two, opening her up. After one gasp, her throat closed in. The tentacle seemed to expand, thickening as it ventured further.

This, what Karl did to her, was monstrous and yet she groaned and shuddered, her belly heavy with desire. A want she'd never known burgeoned.

Panic arrived. She'd never done this before. *Never.*

Then she realized what this was all about. What her search for the ten inch schlong was truly about. *My god. Nooo. I've been so stupid!*

"Shh. You're not."

Karl kissed her nape and wrapped her up tight with more tentacles, tight, tighter, squishier, making her feel...feel, *wanted*, taken, possessed. Like a vacant building where a whole busload of squatters has moved in all at once.

So novel, she'd never felt wanted.

"You're wanted." He moved aside the tentacle over her mouth and kissed her, hard, relentless, until she parted her lips and let his tongue in. When he'd aroused her to the point that she was groaning into his mouth, he slid the tentacle back into place. "Now, sweet, sweet woman, I'm going to fill every hole with me until you're bursting."

The image that gave her, but she couldn't stop squirming against his body.

Too much. Too soon. *I mustn't.*

Although a tentacle was already worming into her pussy, she tried to clamp down and make herself impenetrable.

"Not happening, girl," he murmured. "I'm in there. And here too." Another tentacle, a third? How the hell did she know? Maybe he had a million of them, she wondered, as yet another slipped around in her wetness then probed her other hole. Ever so tenderly, it opened her and surged inward.

She gaped, struggling for a moment, and the mouth tentacle took advantage of her parted lips and moved into her mouth. Saliva pooled. She surrendered and simply *felt*.

Fuck.

Sensations, ones she'd never thought to feel, overwhelmed her in a rippling, rhythmic tide.

Hotness. Man. Tentacles everywhere. She craved it all. The slithering. The pushing. The pulling and prying her apart. It was making her one with him. Her spine strained back as two more encircled her breasts and cradled them in a firm grip. Isolated and embraced, blood built in them and thumped through her with each beat of her heart.

Lust pumped and rippled into the essence of her being.

"Yes, Virginia. I've got you. I told you, you'd be mine." His kisses on her shoulder and neck became more savage – biting, painful, but she shuddered, feeling an orgasm build.

The onslaught commenced.

No crevice or cavity or part of her was not taken by him, was not cradled, squashed, perverted, or penetrated. The ones within her moved as far in as they could possibly go and began to pulse. They swelled bigger, then shrank, then grew again. On top of her clit, inside her pussy, they shuddered against her inner flesh – amplifying her desire.

She wanted *more*, and moaned and writhed in his monstrous embrace.

"I'm in you. I'm around you. I *am* you, Virginia. And you are me." His voice was close to her ear. That too seemed inside her. Warm man voice, vibrating into her.

She arched against his strength, into the beastlike passion of sex, enough to feel her body offering itself to him.

In unison, the tentacles thrust into her.

Fuck.

She came, shuddering, shaking, crying out against the smothering thing in her mouth, all of her pulsing around the tentacles intruding into her female parts.

Her heart pounded crazily. She panted, her thoughts swimming.

And he hadn't even done anything to her clit this time.

"That," he whispered, "is next."

It began again. The suckers played with, licked and sucked onto, every one of her most sensory laden places, tasting and stirring her clit and her nipples, fucking her in time to the sucks.

Another orgasm thundered in, lightning seemed to flash, even through the tentacle over her eyes. The floor beneath her soles shook. She screamed and gasped, and screamed some more.

She soon lost count of how many holes he'd penetrated – more than she thought she had. Tentacle sex seemed to invent new places to fuck. Only her nose remained unpoked.

She really needed to brush up on her maths.

Her throat was raw by the time he stopped and she was limp, sweat sodden, and softly moaning. Drool dripped from her chin. Her limbs trembled as he let her down from the ropes and untangled himself from her. He lowered her to the rugs and lay by her side, stroking her with his hands and tentacles while she recovered. Warm. Tired. Her eyelids drifted closed.

"That was so wrong," she muttered, though snuggling back into him. Spooning was nice. Why hadn't she tried this before?

Because my friends don't have tentacles, her inner voice suggested snidely.

Oh yeah. That.

Rude, though. She shot her inner voice with a tranquillizer dart and fastened it to the corner with duct tape.

Dumb-ass voice.

He kissed her ear, brushed away sweaty hair from her neck. "Yes, why, Virginia? I know you figured this out. You were scared?"

Was this the tender, after sex, get-to-know-you session?

"Yes. It is."

"Stop with the mind reading, Karl."

"Sorry."

"I did figure it out. I think. My quest for the ten inch schlong was all a façade, a way to avoid..."

"What?"

She sighed and wriggled her head into a better spot against his shoulder. "This. Intimacy. Sex. I was avoiding it by making sex impossible. Only I still haven't exactly done it, you know."

"Yes, you have." He sounded indignant. "I fucked you."

Dangerous Bob stepped up, looming above them.

Virginia shrieked, a little, enough to show she was modest, and tried to cover her breasts, no, no, her pussy. No, her breasts. *Wait. Oh crap.* She grabbed a tentacle that had appeared and used it down there, slapping it on to cover herself.

Karl laughed.

Damn. Who cared? He'd seen all of her, and seen her being thoroughly molested while having the best orgasms of her life.

"Fuckitty. Grr. Fuckerate." *No, sir, you didn't. You never used your sex tentacle on Miss Virginia.*

Miss Virginia? Since when did Bob become like a snooty-nosed butler?

She craned her head back to speak to Karl. "What is a sex tentacle?"

CHAPTER 8

"A sex tentacle, or copulating tentacle, is the one I mate with." His tone sounded curious, as if what Bob had said had started a train of thought. "It's like this one, except it's purple." He waved one before her eyes.

She couldn't tear her eyes away. Orange, it was a dark and pretty orange, but he'd said purple? Her lifelong goal was in sight. Almost. The suckers pulsated, mesmerizing her. She was still processing what had happened. Who'd have thought tentacle sex would be her first? Or so awe-inspiring. She shivered.

"Dangerous Bob is correct. Maybe that's why I still have this need to take you again? With the others, once I was done with them, it was easy to throw them to the portal."

"What?" She struggled up onto her elbow then turned to face him. At least he looked normal, apart from the couple of tentacles still curling out from behind his back. "Are you saying you might not have wanted me if you'd stuck your sex tentacle up my...my –"

"Cunt?"

She gasped. "Dirty!"

He grinned and looked evil. "You think that's dirty, innocent girl? But to answer you, maybe."

"Where did you put that one then?" The idea of him having a special one was making her a little crazy with lust again. Why, she wasn't sure. Though what the hell did he have in his pants? Was that where his copulating tentacle was?

"I put it," he tapped her chin, "in there."

Virginia snapped her mouth shut and he smiled broadly.

If that hadn't been drool running down her chin, she'd...she'd... "Fuck, that's hot."

"We can do it again that way, soon. This means you're still a virgin, except for your pretty little mouth." He smiled then lowered his voice. "I'm going to put it in there again soon and make you suck me off."

"*Uhh.*" This man was hotter than a bike's exhaust in the Nevada desert.

Her inner voice stirred. She knew what it wanted her to do. For once, she agreed, so she sat up on her heels and took a deep breath.

"Cyndie. Where is she? Before I will allow you to do anything to me ever again, I want you to bring her back."

"You what?" His eyes narrowed. "I can do what I want to you. Forever and ever."

Oooh. That sounded fucking hot too. *Be good. Do not crack.* "Not necessarily. One day, I'd get free. But I'll agree to be yours, if you bring the other women back."

All the tentacles zipped away and he rose to his feet, strolled over to where his shirt lay, slowly put it on then buttoned it.

"I think I can get that agreement from you anyway." He picked up a remote control from the console and pressed a button. A screen on the console came to life as he walked back to her and hauled her to her feet. "My Virginia, I have taken the liberty of bringing your entire apartment back here."

On the screen a room showed and it was indeed packed with her belongings. Dresses hung in cupboards, shoes were set out below.

"Ohmigod. How'd you figure out my address? And how did you get it here so fast?" She grabbed at her hair with both hands and tugged. Was this real?

"Money talks. So does a pack of violently inclined bikers." Another screen flicked on. "I also have your pet canary." *Flick.* "Your car." *Flick.* "And your grandma is on standby."

The last screen showed her grandmother beating Crank about the ears with her handbag. She winced. Poor Crank.

"It's a *no* to the last one." She spluttered. Her belly did flip flops. This was true love! "*Awww.* You stalked me!"

"Yes," he said proudly. "I did. Will you have my babies?"

She stiffened. She must stand firm even though her lip quivered.

"Karl, I would love to have your little monster babies but you have to bring back the other women. My conscience would never forgive me if I didn't insist on this. No matter how much you stalking me and tying me up and forcing me to have sex has made me love you."

Her heart went pitter pat again at the very thought of how much trouble he'd gone to.

His shoulders slumped. "It's impossible. I can't do it."

Crap.

Dangerous Bob piped up, waving a bottle at them from behind the console where he'd apparently found a kitchen nook and a supply of wine. "Fuckitty. Rrrr. Grr." *The reverse switch is right here under the toaster, sir.*

"It is?" Karl's eyebrows climbed for the ceiling, but stopped short. "Oh good. *That* switch. Fine. Do it then."

Dangerous Bob pulled something and the rug swirled madly then was blown into the air. The red eye beneath turned green and naked women began popping out and rolling across the floor. Last of all Cyndie crawled out along with a few hopping rabbits. Dazed, she picked up a rabbit and stroked it.

"Cyndie!" Virginia ran to her, avoiding the humming portal, and dragged her to safety. "Where have you been? What was it like in another dimension?"

The poor woman could barely speak. "Hairdressers. Big stone things. Gargoyles. Letter boxes. *Mmm.*" She nodded as if she'd delivered the ten commandments.

Karl squeezed Virginia's shoulder. "See! Done."

"She's a bit weird."

"Jet lag."

"I guess. She always was a bit odd. There was that time she wouldn't lend me her hairdryer." She leaned her head back against his chest. "Thank you, Karl."

"Nothing is too much for you, my sweet captive."

"*Mmm.*" She smiled and let him hold her ever so tightly, like he was scared she might run out the door like all the other women were now doing. "I'm yours forever now. I've rescued Cyndie, even if she is lacking a few brain cells."

His grip got even tighter and he squeezed her ass where his mark still stung. "Yes, you have, and you are mine now, for all eternity."

"Sir?"

Who was that? *Crap*. She felt her eyes widen. Dangerous Bob had spoken a real word.

He stepped closer. Over his arm lay a black cat suit and in the other hand was a pistol.

"What is it?" Karl tensed. "I see. Those are for you, Virginia. Before this story can end, you need to have worn the black latex cat suit and held the gun. It's contractual. On the book cover. Though next time they'd better get my tentacle color right. Or else."

His mouth quirked in a knowing smile and he stared past her, as if someone was there, watching them.

Creepy. Ice cold crept over her skin and she shivered, then she checked. No one was there, of course.

But she could feel the draw of this, the rightness, and she went to Bob and took the clothes then slipped on the suit, even though when she zipped it up she almost burst an eyeball.

"Tight," she wheezed.

"Sexy." Karl's crotch was quite...bulgier.

Feeling coquettish, she turned and waggled her butt, posing with the gun out like a female secret-agent super spy.

"Wow. Come here so I can take it off you again with my tentacles. Or maybe I'll just tear it open in the right places." His tone was downright snarly, like he'd rip open the jugular of any man who so much as looked at her.

"You beast." This time it was her purring.

"That's me." His smile dripped with raw and bloody ferocity and the promise of dangerous sex.

Ohhh, those black irises. This cat suit had superpowers. If only she could breathe in it.

All three of them observed her, even Cyndie who still stroked the rabbit. It was rumbling and its eyes glowed red.

She stared. "You might want to put down the rabbit, Cyndie. I think it's about to do something. Like explode?"

"No." She tossed her head. "It's a good rabbit. Safe. Wait until you see it vibrate."

"Ahh. It's one of those." So that's where those rabbits came from.

The rabbit rumbled louder.

Karl held out his hand to her. "Come to me, my virgin. Our story is done."

"Wait!" A brilliant idea had sprung up. "Group photo! Yes?"

They all shrugged then agreed. Even the rabbit nodded.

Dangerous Bob tossed her his phone and she set it on the console with a five second timer on, dashed over to them and posed fast, with the gun up. Then she ran back to the phone to check.

The one photo enlarged to fill the screen. There they all were looking, by turns, stunned, sexy, menacing, and weird.

She groaned. "Bob!" His fingers showed in a *V*, behind the rabbit's head.

His chuckle and murmured, good-natured, *fuckerrrr rabbit*, made her grin back at him.

"Rabbit ears, Bob?" Karl rolled his eyes. "Done now, Virginia?"

"Almost," she said quietly, staring pointedly at his groin. "There is one last thing. I still haven't seen your...your ten inch tentacle schlong."

"You think you deserve to?" He arched one eyebrow then the other. Slowly he unzipped his fly.

"Yes. Yes I do. Please? Please, Karl. I *need* to! I'll even get down on my knees and beg if you want me too!"

He smirked. "Oh we'll try that too. Just you wait." Then he unzipped himself all the way.

Virginia took a step closer to see, unfortunately she also blocked the reader's view of Karl's lower regions. There was a loud thump and the floor trembled as if a small earthquake had struck.

"Big enough for you, sweet lady?"

She gasped, choking a little. "Oh my goodness, Karl. That's not ten inches! That's more like ten pounds! No wonder my mouth was so full!"

Fade...to black.

Except for the rabbit's glowing red eyes, which then also fade. The purring ceases.

Cyndie shrieks. "My rabbit's died!"

Dangerous Bob growls a few choice fucks. *It's just the batteries.*

And so The Quest for the Rabbit's Batteries begins.

STRUM

Yet another erotic parody where a light is shone on all the dirty, crazy, squishy things dwelling in your romances.

When a stag party goes terribly wrong, Virginia Chaste loses her memory of all the best bits of her fiancé, Karl whatsisface. She awakens with her tongue stuck to the castle floor, a suspicion that someone kissed her, a missing fiancé, and no idea what will happen next. Luckily Dangerous Bob can show her the way.

All she has to do is join Zagan Grimm, rock star and demon, he of the radioactive cock, to retrieve the ultimate sex book, the Necrosexi-texmexicon from the depths of the Zon, then she can get her fiancé back, even if she'd rather sell his castle and make a million dollars.

Then she absolutely has to remember not to have a spectacular, tentacular ménage with Zagan and Karl whatsisface.

With so many things to remember, Virginia may forget the last one.

Yes, a big, fat warning to all those with pristine, well-vacuumed minds: Here Be Tentacles.

Once Upon a Time,
there was much controversy about exactly what covers the mighty
Zon,
aka Amazon,
would accept on its misty and awesome internet bookshelves.

Many wondrous things were rumored to have been banished to the
deserted Nether lands
tits, cocks, bums, and even nipples.

This book, Strum,
attempts to make sense of the laws of the Zon in the same way Alice
made sense of Wonderland,
with a good helping of illegal drugs
and many weird animals that smile at you before they eat you.

CHAPTER 1

Virginia awoke, and after several aborted attempts, managed to open her eyelids. Her tongue was stuck to the floor with semi-dried drool. Someone was shaking her. Who?

His name surfaced from the swampy garbage heap steaming up the inside of her brain. She unstuck her tongue.

"Dangerwous..." She tried again. "Bob?"

He grunted, shifting forward to help her sit up. There was a glass in his hand and he offered her a few sips.

Virginia blinked and shook her head. She was in a bedroom. Hers, she figured. The quilt, the desk – familiar. Ditto, the cross-eyed seagull on the window sill – the one that always fell off when the phone rang.

"What? Is this my..." Things blurred.

Dangerous Bob swore severely then put a finger to his lips. He helped her to the bed and steadied her when she sat on the edge. Her feet felt miles away, so did her head.

"What happened?" She raised her hand to feel a sore spot on her head and was surprised at the glinting diamond ring on one finger. "What's this? I'm engaged?"

Bob sighed and for the first time she could recall, he looked flustered. He let out a whole string of fucks, interspersed with some craps, shits, and words from another language that were also likely profane. Some of them turned into real words in her mind.

She thought through the translation that always came with his swearing. She'd become so used to Bob's odd talent of talking through swearing that it didn't faze her.

Do you remember what happened?

"Only that there was a stag party and I went down to tell them to be quiet. Then...nothing. And I seem to remember a green thing whizzing past."

You remember being engaged to Karl? Karl gave you the ring.

Her memories served up images. Karl? Nice man. Nice. Calm. Handsome. Sexy. All of the memories were like pictures. She knew him as a friend and that was it.

"Engaged? No. So, I'm engaged to him?"

"Fuckitty fuck. Fiirrr. Grr. Fuckitty."

What he'd said was so mindboggling she had to repeat it to make sense of it.

"I was supposed to be married later today? The wedding was supposed to be *this* day?"

He nodded.

And this was Karl's castle.

"Oh fuck. I can barely remember him." She leaned back on her hands and saw the ring down there. She'd woken up on the day she was to be married to a man she could barely remember, but she *wasn't* married to him. All she had was this ring.

"Where is he? Something has happened to him, hasn't it?" Damn, she should be feeling unhappy. And she was, but it was a vague and weird unhappiness, like she'd lost something but didn't know what it was.

Bob nodded for a long time, a sad expression deforming his already somewhat ugly face.

Virginia grimaced. Cheer the man up fast or she'd be puking. "It's okay, Dangerous Bob. We'll find him. I mean he's here somewhere? In the castle?"

This time he shook his head.

Wait. She was living in Karl's castle but they weren't married yet...

"Ohmigod." She put her hand over her mouth. "We didn't have sex or anything, did we?"

The fixed grin on Bob's face said it all.

"I lost my virginity and I can't remember it? This is way worse than waking up unconscious..."

He interrupted. *Technically when you're awake, you can't be unconscious.*

She fluttered her hand. "Worse than waking up and not

remembering not getting married to a man I don't remember meeting! Way worse. I think. I'm not sure what I just said...but it's awful!" She buried her face in her hands and spoke around her fingers. "My quest for the ten inch schlong is ruined."

While she sobbed he patted her on the back, and as her crying ebbed he began to explain what he'd discovered. The string of swearing went on for so long that she knew he'd have an entire posse of girls clinging to him by now if there'd been any nearby. Being immune to Bob's girlnip cursing had its advantages. At least she could simply be his friend.

Damn she hoped Karl was ten inches. Maybe she could get out of this marriage if he wasn't?

She'd better listen to Bob.

He rambled on, carefully pacing his swearing so she understood.

What he said surprised her.

Wow. Maybe she was still, sort of, a virgin...because Karl hadn't penetrated her with his mating...*what?* Tentacle? Couldn't be. She'd mistranslated that *fuck*, obviously. But there seemed an out. They mustn't have had proper sex after all. Maybe she'd only done a BJ? Did that make her half a virgin?

Bob had found everyone in the castle unconscious, as she had been, even the cleaners. He'd woken them all. One of them recalled her returning to her room by herself, and some recalled seeing a strange, green, sparkling book fly through the hallways and out a window before everything went blank.

Karl was missing along with the Sea Wolves – she could remember *them* – and along with the portal. No portal. That apparently was important since the portal went to another dimension and Bob seemed to think, because of markings in the portal room, that they'd all gone through it at the stag party.

"Uh-huh." She tapped her teeth. "And the book?"

From the sightings by the cleaners and the direction of travel, it came out of the portal.

"Can we rescue them? Get them back? Make another portal?"

"Fuck."

Startled, she drew back. That was one big fat *no.*

Something about this whole scenario was familiar. A castle full of asleep people. One man coming to wake them. A fairy tale... Sleeping Beauty!

She stared at him suspiciously. Had he kissed her? To wake her? Then she remembered her drool-stuck tongue. *Eww.*

If he *had* kissed her, he deserved a medal.

Her potential but forgotten husband was gone.

After a short mourning period, *one second, two seconds, three seconds,* it was time to be practical.

"So!" She clapped her hands together. "How much will the castle bring on the real estate market? And do you want half?"

His scowl was immense, deep, and a little frightening.

Perhaps he had other ideas? "What?"

Stay.

When he returned later that day he told her to get ready for a journey and dumped a small suitcase on the bed then opened it.

Pack.

"Why? Where are we going?"

Hands on hips, he set out some facts. He had, apparently, been googling, reading, talking, more googling.

We're all fucked. That book was the Necrosexi-texmexicon. It's evil incarnate.

"Okayyy. Mmm. Bad. Yup." She had no clue.

But she figured incarnate evil was probably worse than other sorts of evil.

Funny how she could remember everything about Dangerous Bob. She had such a convenient amnesia. And this story would be so damned hard to tell without her knowing him.

Though ugly as a stick of exploded ugliness with his scarred face and real wire, wire-brush hair, Dangerous Bob was a loyal and a mostly good man, when he wasn't being excessively violent. He was a solid presence. He was a man who swore a lot but he got things done when they needed to be done.

Right now, it sounded like he wanted to do things.

"Where is the book going?"

She took in the rumbled swearing, turning his words over in her mind.

To the Zon, where all things of momentous importance go.

Momentous was not a word she would've imagined Bob as even knowing let alone using. It was up there with incarnate.

*Copies of all the books in existence are at the Zon. Plus Lawn ornaments. Movies. Sex toys. The Zon is a dangerous place. If the

Necrosexi-texmexicon makes it to the heart of the Zon, the world may cease to exist as it is now.

"Cool." She nodded brightly. "So you're going to go fetch it?"

He slammed shut the suitcase and locked it. *We are.*

Damn, there'd been so much dialogue, she hadn't put anything in the suitcase. "Umm. Bob? I need to put in bras and panties, at least."

Bob blushed bright red.

After she packed properly, he made her kick off her heels, shove back the sleeves of her shirt, and repeat some words, because apparently, this was what the old her would've said.

She began. "We're going to restore the Necrosexi...fucking thingicon to where it came from if I have to shove it down a toilet and flush it to get it there?"

He nodded eagerly and encouraged her to keep going.

"Time for me to be mean and kick some ass?" Bob was so into this. Maybe he thought it would jog her memory? The next bit was strange but she said it with gusto and a fist swipe to make him happy. "The things a girl has to do to get tentacle fucked on her wedding day!"

There was that tentacle word again. Nope. Saying that hadn't jogged a thing.

As they left the room she took a last look. She could sell this place later if things went back-assward.

Oh wait. The world was going to cease to exist. Maybe they did need to kick some butt.

She paused with her hand on the door knob. A memory barged in. The stag party. She'd seen a man.

He'd made the world screech to a halt. The raging stag-party music had gone far, far away. Ravens had appeared, flying in circles, cawing in a distant sort of way – which was really weird since this was inside a room.

Most of all, she remembered *Him*.

A muscular man in a red shirt wearing black skinny jeans, aviator sunglasses, and a multitude of flame tattoos. White hair, and the flames on his skin had writhed as if alive.

An aisle of rock had crackled from him to her. The surface beneath her feet had trembled. The room had spun and blurred.

In that instant, she'd known that it meant either impending doom or she'd found a heart-sent lover – a lover who was to be with her forever until the end of time. A lover who would die with her, his arms wrapped about her, never letting go as their ship sank and sank into the cold, quiet, depths of the ocean. Spiraling down, drowning...

Like the Titanic, but worse.

That had been pretty creepy. Her inner voice, in the back of her mind, had made a note not to ever go on a cruise.

The ravens had cawed and circled some more.

She recalled thinking that getting the bird shit off the rug was going to be hell then blackness had rained down.

Heart-sent lover? Whoever he was, he couldn't be. She already had one of those: Karl whatsisface. If she could find him. The alternate dimensions really needed a Lost and Found department.

CHAPTER 2

Dangerous Bob throttled back and the bike glided to a halt outside the entrance gate to the Rockschlock gig. Strobing lights and thunderous riffs blasted from a distant stage somewhere at the far end of the huge conference hall. She'd been surprised when she'd seen the address. Purgatory playing at a dismal hall out in the suburbs? Crazy.

Here was the man that Bob said they needed. Zagan Grimm. A major planet in her universe of rock stars. The man, himself. Only Bob thought he was a demon. Those – rock star and demon – seemed a little mutually opposite, but hey, she wasn't arguing with a man with an artificial cock who possibly ate bricks for breakfast.

Virginia hopped off the bike, clutching her bulging handbag to her side. The lines of people trying to get in were atrocious and as hungry looking as a snake waiting to gulp down a mouse.

"Fuckitty," Bob murmured. He knew the potency of his swearing. Girl attractant el supremo. If he spoke too loudly, they'd be knee-deep in squealing girls.

"I'll be okay." She inhaled, determined. "You sure you can't come in?"

He jerked his chin at Security, who were sweeping everyone with metal detectors. Then he smacked his palm onto his groin and shook his head.

His artificial cock would never get past that security check. This was her mission, her problem, from here on in.

"Point taken." She was on her own, except for her wits, her wiles, her mostly virgin pussy, and the card Bob had given her. "I'll text you."

He nodded, switched on the bike but stayed there, watching, as she walked away. The lycra of her octopus motif tights gripped her so firmly, they seemed likely to cut off circulation to her legs. It occurred to her to pull down the pink T-shirt and show some cleavage, or she could maybe waggle her ass, if she wasn't worried about popping out somewhere. No. She wasn't a loose woman. She'd get past security without that.

"Whoah, bitch!" A man's voice from the queue. She put her nose in the air. "Look at that octo-pussy! Show us what you got in there, girl!"

That did it. She focused on him and glared. "Shut your filthy mouth!"

"What? Have you seen where that octopussy has *his* mouth? He's eating you out, slut. If you don't like him, I'll do it!"

The crowd laughed.

She fumed. Wearing these had been a bad idea. She'd thought they'd make her look like a rock chick. Sadly, the octopus did seem to be sucking on her crotch. Bob's taste was a bit lewd. She held up a middle finger, waggling it at the bald guy with the big mouth, a few feet ahead. "You, you..."

Her smart ass reply died away.

As she approached, she lowered her aim and looked at his groin but her normal schlong-hunting and appraising hobby had lost its attraction.

Hah. A seven point five incher. And sadly she was half a virgin. A woman in no man's land. *Or was that no-cock land? Who cared how long his schlong was.* Though, *hmmm*, she tilted her head, and ran through the calculations. The man needed her aid.

"Twenty-nine point two seconds to ejaculation and a problem with maintaining an erection? See a doctor about that, mister."

"What?" His lip trembled and he shrank back into the crowd.

She sighed and walked onward without any further comments about his schlong. She was adrift. Without her complete and undisputed virginity, the world had lost something, a spark of sorts.

As she went past, a few of the men added width to their leers, patently staring at her pussy, correction, her octopussy. Behind her she heard a not-so-subtle snarl from Bob. Some hard looking men moved his way. If anyone could take care of themselves, it was Dangerous Bob.

Ignore. Ignore. Ignore. She kept going.

As she approached the gate, bypassing the queues, the smell of spilled stale beer tainted the air.

A security guard held up his hand, palm out. "Sorry ma'am, you need to get into line."

"You need to look at this." She handed him the gold-edged card.

Once Bob had figured out this was who they had to see, he'd tried contacting Zagan only to be repeatedly knocked back. This was their last resort, a black market, backstage pass to a Purgatory gig.

The guard tilted an eyebrow and added his leer to the crowd's. "It's not a backstage pass but it will get you in, if you go around the side to the right. Next gate." He wiggled the card.

"It's not?" In the alternating flash of intense lights then gloom, she couldn't make out the writing. "What is it then?"

He grinned and held it up to her eyes.

BACK ENTRY PASS. Then in smaller writing: *The holder guarantees anal sex to Skoll Blade.*

Her mouth fell open.

"Yep, use this pass and know Skoll expects to use your pretty little ass good."

Jeez. Mouth firm, eyes hard, she said angrily and perhaps a little too loudly, "Let me in this way then."

"No. Not a hope. If you ain't got a ticket and you want in, you sacrifice your butt. Which is it? You're holding up the fucking line."

Just as she opened her mouth to say something bad, a motor bike revved loudly and shouting erupted.

"Fuck!" The guard sprinted past her along with his three cohorts.

A crowd milled around where Dangerous Bob was flailing about with fists and his trusty four by two...*where in hell had that come from*...laying out his attackers with precision and grace. The roar intensified as the guards joined in, but Bob only hooted and waved to her when he noticed her watching.

"Awww." She smiled. Sweet man. He was making the fight last so it was a diversion for her. Ah least he was having fun. She swiveled on the heels of her stilettos, managed not to fall over on her nose, then sauntered in through the unattended gate.

CHAPTER 3

The first step Virginia took inside the hall brought her smack bang up against a man with a face like a creature from a dog pound. Squarest jaw ever, slightly jutting out, with beady, deep-set eyes. To be precise, she'd gone smack bang, nose-first, into his white-shirted, Security-tagged chest – a chest that was so broad she'd need an airline ticket to circumnavigate it.

Past his shoulder was where she needed to be. Smoke and too many multi-colored floodlights made the stage at the far end of the hall seem to float on a fog of agitated, waving fans. As the song ended, a high-pitched decrescendo riff punctuated the drama of the moment. The crowd screamed, roared, and thumped its feet on the seating stands to either side and above her.

She blinked and resisted the urge to retreat, or to get out something long and nasty and poke him with it.

He smiled down at her.

Eeek. She sucked in a startled breath.

Teeth. Big. Sharp. *Pointy.* Teeth.

Who the fuck in psychofuckadelic land had triangular teeth? Cross out the something long and nasty, she needed a cage and a bunch of zoo keepers.

She was used to all Karl's Sea Wolves bikers, most of whom, despite their liking for leather and motorcycles, could shift to become scary sea-living monsters.

Could this guy shift? And if so, what was he, a shark?

"Where do you think you're going, lil tasty thing?" The rumbles from his voice made the floor quake, though that was possibly her knees knocking.

Sometimes her mouth did bad things before she could stop it. "You file those in your spare time, or did your mama have intimate relations with a lumber mill?"

Inwardly she was pleased. *Good mouth*. You didn't show fear before guys like this or they stomped on you.

He chuckled. "Har har de har. No." He leaned in and sniffed her. "Oh, baby. You smell good. I eat things that smell this good."

Oh my. Next time she'd sew her lips together.

"Either you show me that ticket you must have somewhere on you." His gaze lazily perused most of her from breasts to legs, and back to her breasts. "I can even help you find it. Or I get to throw you out. Or..."

Fuckitty, as Bob would say. "Or what?"

As soon as the words left her mouth, she realized she shouldn't have said them. She'd admitted she wasn't here legitimately.

"Or you let me fuck you behind the stands and I'll let you go watch the show after."

Making a small unhappy noise only made him focus on her sharply. If she twitched, he'd pounce. He came closer, aiming to edge her under the framework of the stand.

"You don't say nothing and I'll take that as a yes. Mm Mmm. I'm going to like this. I'm big so you're going to have to spread those pretty legs a looong way so's I can get in deep in your wet, tight pussy."

"I'm taken," she squeaked out.

"Yeah, you will be soon."

Horrible man.

Would he reject her if she told him she might not be so tight anymore after coping with tentacles? Not that she believed Bob. The man had been smoking something. He actually thought Karl had tentacles.

Her thoughts scurried about like lost sheep.

She stared at him, trying to think, and sucking on her lip like it was a favorite lollipop. She'd broken herself of the biting-the-lip habit. Maybe she needed a patch. Like a nicotine patch, only with a mouth instead...

A lip patch. Yeah.

"You want some of *this*? My deadly trouser snake?" He came so close she could hear the tinkle of metal under his shirt. From glimpses of something shiny, he was wearing a ton of silver necklaces. "It bites."

Despite his words being vile, her pussy was flooding like a basement room with a busted pipe. Alpha men always made her go all squishy.

You are disgusting, her inner voice muttered. *And that busted pipe analogy? Get a plumber before I throw up.*

She didn't have time for this. Her inner voice needed a smackdown now and then.

"Shut up or I duct tape you again," she sieved the words between her teeth, unintentionally out loud.

Oh shit. He was looking weirded out. Her mind went quiet.

Then her inner voice giggled-snorted.

Dammit. "Shhh!"

"Are you okay?" The man peered at her worriedly.

"What?" Virginia spat out. "You don't like crazy women?"

He shrugged.

"Take a look at this. *Baby.*" Exasperated beyond hope of normality, she whipped out the Back Entry pass.

"You know what that is?" The stock issue leer, that all the men here tonight seemed to have bought, sneaked onto his face.

"Yes! I do. Take me to your fucking leader."

"Okay." He shrugged again, though the leer only faded to a know-it-all smile. "Follow me." He grabbed her hand and set off for the stage with her in tow. "I'm not risking you changing your mind. I'm T, by the way. You?"

Change of agenda. Now it was introductions? She struggled to keep up without tripping over her own heels. If she fell from this height, she'd likely burn up in the atmosphere.

"That's it, just T? I'm Virginia Chaste."

"No shit." He chuckled. "You won't be chaste for much longer. The T is for Tyrone. Last name Rex. Mr. T. Rex if we're being formal."

No. No, no. no. For the first time she noticed how short his arms were. Functional but short.

"You're not..."

He looked at her suspiciously. "Not what?"

"Not..." She couldn't say it.

"Catholic? No. Circumcised?" He grinned. "Not that either."

And all the while inside her head, her inner voice was hopping up and down, screaming, *Dinosaur. Dinosaur!* Like some host on a kid's show before they broke into song.

For once, she was too stunned to smack it.

Maybe he didn't know he could shift?

Maybe he couldn't?

Yeah, she was dreaming up nightmares for no reason. She guessed having a theoretical tentacle monster fiancé could do that to you.

Even so, one thought blasted across her brain, as glaring as a highway sign being flattened by a truck.

She'd nearly fucked a dinosaur.

She wouldn't have.

Not really.

Damn. A dinosaur!

Would that make her more a slut than being, *haha*, tentacle fucked did? This was like the chicken and the egg question. The philosophy of fucking monsters.

How big was dino dick?

Wait. Wait, wait, wait. There was a logic problem here. She believed in the possibility of dino-shifters, and recalled the Sea Wolves shifting, but she couldn't conceive of Karl tentacle loving her?

Oh fuck. Shut up with the logic. Tentacle love was just dumb. End of story.

Imagine where they could go though.

Hmm.

Why were her panties even wetter?

CHAPTER 4

Mr. T. Rex made her sit at the front, in a special row of seats.

"Stay there." He leaned in from behind and murmured beside her ear. "You move and my guys have orders to hold you for the cops under charges of stealing. Trust me. We can prove it."

Her indignant gasp didn't impact on him at all and she watched him move away into the crowd.

Dayum. Just because he was top of the food chain.

She was off to the left of the stage but three yards from a bank of speakers high enough to tempt King Kong to climb it with a virgin in his grasp.

The next song began with a strident chord from Zagan's golden Stratocaster that made her brain spring a leak through her ears. His wide-legged, pelvic strutting routine was classic Zagan. His *Sneering Donkeys Spunk Rock* T-shirt, plastered with an image of guitar-playing purple donkeys with nuclear explosions coming out their asses, was classic Purgatory wear.

Why had she not recognized him? It was *He.* Him. The guy at the party. Only this time his eyes were bare of sunglasses, revealing his burning flames contact lenses. As he slashed his hand across the strings and led the band into the heart of the song, his eyes focused on her.

Her breath stopped. Her heart stood still then took off like a cat at a meeting of violin enthusiasts.

With the beat turning the rest of her brains to jelly, she recalled how the floor had crackled toward her. For a moment the stage seemed to shimmy and bow up at the sides as if stretching into a circle with him at the center.

Kinky. Nervously she checked the nearest load-bearing beams. Maybe she should have brought an architect with her?

Psst. Need oxygen.

She breathed and things were sort of okay again. Spiders on the drum kit? Normal for Purgatory. The evil clown, she was reserving judgment on.

The hall turned into a battlefield of ripples and flashes of light, a war of music where the casualties were the audience. Men screamed and swayed in time. A mosh pit formed to the side. Women leaped up and down and danced from the waist up while sitting on their boyfriends' shoulders. Some fainted. Several had their heads spin in circles and their panties burst into flame.

Though boyfriends threw themselves atop the women to smother the flames, from the writhing bodies and the squeals of *ohmigod* and *oooh*, it rarely seemed to work.

Concerned security guards roamed vigilantly with fire extinguishers to put out the fires. A few girls exploded entirely and had to be scraped off the walls.

Mortalities were to be expected at a Purgatory concert.

The show must have taken hours but not once did she take her eyes off Zagan, nor his off hers. They were riveted together like a pair of electrically welded joints on a table. It made for a lot of tripping over power cables onstage, and Zagan almost lost an eye on a mic stand but neither of them seemed able to resist the other.

At the end, when people around her were filing out or screaming for more, she stayed where she was until the place was empty. The band left. Security still watched her and had told her to stay put despite her glares. Then he returned.

Zagan vaulted down to where she sat and held out his hand. "Come with me."

How could she resist? Not only did his irises seem on fire when seen this close, his groin throbbed alarmingly like something in there was desperate to get out. Her mouth dropped open but she resisted drooling.

Must not drool. In the low light, there was a distinct red glow too. The crotch of his black pants glowed? Did he have a glow stick shoved down there? A torch? Would it fit? She tilted her head.

"Come. With me," he repeated, sounding only slightly exasperated at her being fixated on his cock.

Her well-trained schlong detector said unreadable.

A mystery? Hmm. She hated those. The itch to discover what lurked within nibbled at her. She so needed to get this man's pants off. For clinical reasons, of course.

"Sure." She reached for his hand and raised her eyes to meet his.

Boom. Some vital essence of hers recognized his as being the matching element her heart and body needed for life to go on. Butterflies took flight inside her stomach, followed by a herd of antelope and a few flying unicorns in a full-on romantic stampede. Rainbows made their way from pyloric valve to esophagus. Her spleen fainted. It was getting messy in there. She put her palm on her gurgling belly.

Love. Insta-love. She had it bad.

Wasn't there some injection for that?

Tomorrow she should see a doctor.

Virginia inhaled and completed the movement she'd begun what seemed like hours ago. She put her hand in his.

A spark travelled between them. *Zzzap.* Excruciating pain sizzled up her arm. She snatched back her hand and screamed. The lights dimmed. High above, huge purple sparks crackled from ceiling strut to ceiling strut. Some creature let out a startled meow then a hiss.

"What the damn fuck. Shit!" She shook her fingers trying to get the pain to lessen. "Fuck. Was that some crazy static electricity thing, man? Are you wearing velvet or something?"

He was shaking his fingers too. "No, I do not wear velvet. I'm a rock star! Denim. See?" He plucked at his jeans.

When he went to take her hand again, she gingerly accepted. *Phew. Nothing.*

They walked past cleaners shoving piles of litter with brooms. A cat stalked by and shot an accusatory glare at them. Tendrils of smoke rose from its fur. She slowed. Should she get the SPCA to look at the poor kitty? She looked about. Where was the pervert who'd set its fur on fire?

Zagan dragged her onward.

In his dressing room the legendary golden Stratocaster rested against the wall. She eyed it but nothing more. Rumor said it was really gold and that no one except Zagan could pick it up without getting a hernia.

He poured them both a glass of scotch then pulled up a leather lounge chair and sat opposite the sofa she reclined on. From under his brow, through the pale strands of his hair, he looked out.

Such wonderful evil eyes. She shivered.

A caged man, swirling the liquid in the glass, which made his biceps push deliciously at the sleeves of his shirt. His ragged and mostly short, white hair seemed to beg her to run her fingers through it.

His manner suggested a man on the verge of admitting himself to a psychiatric hospital or organizing a worldwide charity for starving orphans, and he stared at the floor so much that she hitched forward to peer at it, to make sure nothing was happening down there.

Zagan Grimm. He was dark. Apart from his white hair. He was brooding. He was a rock star with a guitar and tonsils of gold, and she wanted him so much.

No. Mustn't. Be a good almost-virgin. Not only had she promised Dangerous Bob that she'd behave, she'd promised herself. If she'd been going to marry Karl whatsit, she must have liked him, a lot.

But...instincts were instincts. He was hot and she was female.

With her legs bent and drawn up onto the sofa, she could squeeze her thighs together without making a fuss, and not look like she was desperate to orgasm. She whimpered quietly.

Sexy man. Fuuuuuuck. Her alphabet allowance was depleted. She needed more *U*'s to spell that fuck. Her diamond-hard perky nipples were sawing holes in the front of her T-shirt.

The flames in his eyes flickered and embers fell slowly through the air into the glass, hissing as they hit the golden liquid.

"Wow." To distract herself from the throbbing between her legs, she nodded at the glass. "That's some magic trick."

"It's not one. Did you know the octopus on your tights is eating your pussy?"

His deep voice rumbled like a train bearing down on her, and she was tied to the tracks, unable to escape, waiting for him to run her over.

Do it, baby. Choo, chooo.

"No shit." She smiled, controlling her breathing and trying not to faint. What an intelligent, wonderful man.

"I'm going to lay it all out. I can see you want me. I'm a demon.

You're a mortal. You'll die if I fuck you too much. I'm too much for a sweet girl like you. So..." He heaved in a breath. "Now that that's out of the way, you're going to tell me why you're here and then when we settle that, you'll run away before I drag you onto the floor and ravish you."

Dayum. Be still my beating heart.

Her voice went squeaky. "You'd drag me to the floor and ravish me?"

"If you stay too long, yes." Those eyes turned up the heat by a few thousand degrees.

Amnesia, remember? She had a fiancée. Whatsisface.

I must be good. I must be strong and resist. Besides, there was some small detail about him being a demon and her dying.

She gulped. "I'm engaged."

"I know. I was there. I left early because of you. Once I saw how it was between us. The desire." He set down his glass then took her hand and kissed the palm. "The passion. I also know Karl has left this world. That party was an accident waiting to happen. So why are you here?"

He kissed her wrist and she gave a tiny squeak and felt her womb clenching...which was odd. She was pretty sure it only did that if you were giving birth.

"Good point. He has. Left." Think. What did Dangerous Bob say to do? "I'm here because we need your help to bring him back. Dangerous Bob believes you are the only person capable of finding us, or making us, a new portal."

Pulling her forward, Zagan licked up her wrist all the way to the inside of her elbow. His voice was thick with lust. "You are irresistible." Then he bit.

Eek. Fire swept into her and after torching her mind turned around and scorched southward to her pussy. She was a blazing maelstrom in need of one of those fire extinguishers. Virginia wriggled and attempted to retrieve her elbow from his lips but nothing gave.

"I like this arm where it is." Zagan smiled, showing a row of strong white teeth. "Go on."

She wrestled her breathing into submission.

"He also said to tell you that a special book called the Necrosexi-texmexicon came through the portal into this world just before the portal closed."

"I see." His quiet growl seemed to threaten. 'That's important. Before you can bring back Karl, you will need to have this book. It must return to its world when he returns to this one. Balance is required. But it is an evil book. It contains everything that one can possibly know about sex. Every position. Every toy. Every sexual orientation from trans-Jehovah's Witness to Martian hermaphrodite. Every detail you can imagine, it's in there."

"Sex is evil?"

"No, Virginia, the book is. There's a difference. One more thing. To find the book, are you prepared to sacrifice yourself? Just the once." His grip on her arm tightened.

Ulp. "Why?"

"Because I'm a reject demon, cut loose from Hell. To sense the book, I need power, and I get power by fucking women. It's why they threw me out. I made love too much."

"You sinned? A demon can sin?"

"No. You have it wrong. Sex isn't sin; it's pure goodness. I gooded too much."

Made sense.

If *sacrifice herself* meant what she thought... "I thought it was too dangerous?"

He flipped his hand. "A blow job will do. Better for you, if you don't swallow."

A moment ago, he was too dangerous for her. She mustn't, she mustn't. But the lure of what was behind those glowing pants was slowly unravelling her thoughts.

"You want to," he murmured. "You have to."

He pulled her further until she fell to her knees on the floor. With his gaze pinning her there, despite her resistance, he drew her hand to his zip.

She moaned, anticipating. "I can't! I promised Bob."

"Why can't you? This may save Karl."

The push and pull of conscience and lust was about to tear her apart. Where was her helpful inner voice when she needed guidance?

I'm here, came the dry reply. A rasping sound intruded. *Doing my nails. You sacked me.*

Did not, she told it indignantly.

Did. Stop with the drama, girl. Suck him off. We both know you want to.

Consciences were clearly overrated. Delay him! What was a good question?

"Is this going to kill me?"

"No." He leaned over, put his hand to the back of her head then kissed her forehead, murmuring, so close. "Do it."

With her fingertips clenched by his, she was slowly unzipping him and she couldn't tear her eyes away. The tip of his cock appeared, pulsing deep, incandescent purple, orange, and red, jutting from the top of his boxer shorts. The man...demon, was big. Perhaps too big for her mouth.

"Stop! I'm almost married! Even if I forget what his best bits look like."

But she sighed at the sight of that cock. The thing looked like it might have a life of its own.

"You're not yet. And this is for him."

What an argument. Zagan was a master at debate.

The author typed faster, desperately hoping no one noticed the super-bad almost pun.

"We don't know each other. How do I even know you like me? That seems a minimum requirement." Ignoring the insta-love, which was so convenient she had a feeling someone had fudged the results.

He eyed her, then his twitching cock. Her mouth was barely two inches away from taking him inside...sucking...slurping...doing naughty stuff that needed even more of those dot dot dot ellipsis things.

She licked her lips and wriggled to assuage the ache between her legs.

His reply was soft. Though, gosh darnit, his cock was rather hard. "You want proof? Who do you think awakened you? I went back to see if you were okay. Everyone was asleep."

Oh. My. "You came back." Tears threatened to spill. "Did you kiss me to wake me?"

"Yes." He nodded. "I did, Virginia."

Her mind had a bad habit of thinking things through. Everyone was asleep. She frowned. "And the others? Did you kiss them too?"

"Hell, no! I'm not sick."

Phew. If he'd kissed a shitload of castle people, and then kissed her...ick.

"Listen. I'm radioactive. But you can take one dose." His murmur cut through the last of her resistance. His fingers in her hair crackled with force and just their presence coaxed her to get nearer, to do bad things, to lick him.

The enormous cock swayed there before her, fully erect, waiting for her to close her mouth over it.

"This is fucking huge," she said, awestruck, and going cross-eyed.

Everything about it reminded her of a rocket about to take off. The way it strained upward, swelling with each pulse of his blood. The tortuous veins that ran up its length to the flared tip were like pipelines supplying fuel. The beautiful depth of color – she half expected to see numbers stenciled on the side like *Space Shuttle Number 99*. Plus no cock she'd heard of, and none she'd seen through the multitude of holes she'd drilled in toilet doors, was ever this amazing purplish-red.

For years she'd wanted to see the fabled ten inch purple-headed schlong, and now, one was before her lips.

Like any decent butterfly collector she had this indefinable urge to capture it with a net and smoosh it between a book.

Had she ever had Karl's cock in her mouth? It was odd that she couldn't remember. Could it rival this weapon of mass seduction of Zagan's? The thing looked powerful, lethal. Like, if it went off while she was sucking him, would it blow her head off?

"Do it, girl. Don't hesitate."

"I'm wondering if insurance will cover my head exploding. This is supersize, Zagan. Does it come in extra small or with training wheels?" She twisted her mouth. Not that she really wanted that but it was kinda scary.

"It's the way I roll." He laughed then lowered his voice. "I'm a demon. Trust me, you wouldn't want it smaller. When I come I might not blow your head off but I plan to be so far down your throat, I'll be saying hello to your pussy."

She eyed him. Inspiring confidence was obviously not his strong suit.

"You think too much." Then he grabbed her and shoved, demanding entry, sliding his cock in through her stretched lips. "There."

She had to open more and more as the blunt thing pushed slowly into her mouth. The head slid, prodded, and despite her gagging, travelled inward. Her teeth grazed him as she sank lower and lower, his length gliding over her tongue, sliding on her spit.

Breathing through her nose seemed essential. The things one learned by doing. She made a gurgling noise, and encouraged him to pull out by trying to move her head.

"Good girl." He groaned, took a double handful of her hair, and forced her down onto him another half inch.

He tasted of toasted coconut. Her vision started to blur.

He let her up and she gasped. Had he never heard of breathing?

"The deeper I go, the more you take of me, the more power my balls get from this. Suck me. Lick me. Let me in all the fucking way."

Power to his balls? Somehow, she figured he didn't mean crystal ones.

But was that the truth? If he said it to all his girlfriends...if she found out he didn't really need a BJ. She shot him a sour look.

If the man couldn't harness the power of the sun after this, she was smacking him.

She curled her tongue and caressed the underside, slurping well, pleased at his long groan.

The rhythm intensified as his enormous rocket to the heavens delved into her mouth. Her jaw started to ache but still he thrust in and out, holding her hair to make her do it the way he wanted. Saliva dribbled past her lips and down the now red-hot shaft. She swore she heard sizzling noises. Steam rose from his pants. The pulse in those thick blood vessels hummed against her tongue.

Zagan hummed too and she knew he must be looking at what he was making her do. This was sexy, powerful, and so arousing. She was sure she needed to come almost as much as he did.

"Yes. Fuck, yes," he gasped and he rammed his cock deeper down her throat, choking her again. The pump of his cum as it erupted sent a thrill, a buzz, through the flesh filling her mouth and she swallowed convulsively, feeling cum spurt against the back of her throat.

We have liftoff!

Hot and burning. It mightn't be rocket fuel, but it was radioactive.

Jeez, the things she did for...herself.

She couldn't deny it; she'd liked doing that. When he extracted his cock from her mouth, she sat there on her knees with her eyes mostly closed, clouded in steam and licking her lips of the last of his taste.

"Come here, Virginia." He pulled her up onto his lap and stuck his hand down her tights. "Let's see what this octopus is so fascinated by. Girl, you are so fucking sexy." His hand anchored into the hair at her nape and he dragged her head back and kissed her fully on the mouth. She moaned breathlessly, hypnotized by his flaming eyes and the possessive touch of his mouth on hers.

She drew away a fraction of an inch, her lips brushing his as she spoke.

"Wait. Karl..."

"He's not here. You need this." Then he smothered any further protests with his mouth.

His fingers below alternated between slipping up and down her soaking wet slit and around and around her clit like some tantalizing game of tag where her clit was home base. At first she strived to get away but passion overrode her misgivings. She writhed. She pushed her pelvis up at him then compulsion arrived and, moaning, she rode his fingers hard, grinding.

Closer. *More*. She gasped. *Oh fuck. More*.

When she tried her to unstick her mouth from his to say something, he kissed her harder, made her bring her tongue into the game.

Their tongues dueled like a pair of the three musketeers doing sword practice. En guard. Riposte. Parry.

Her arousal rose, built to the edge of the edge of a big mile-deep chasm and when she fell she was going to need some damn good wings. One of his fingers parted her lower lips and drove up inside her. She arched and came, spasming around his hand, gasping into his mouth. The luscious joy expanded into her mind and carried everything away except it, the O, making her feel, and strain upward with her thighs, and grab at the nearest hard muscle. With her eyes rolled back, she keened until she collapsed back into the real world and found her mouth still open, screaming quietly. He kissed her once more.

"Done, beautiful?"

"That. Was incredible."

"I am a demon. A sex demon."

Wow. Panting, with her forehead tucked into his chest, she clutched his shoulders. Whatever the rules were for this sport, she needed to get a copy of the manual, ASAP.

CHAPTER 5

"Hiya. Want some? This is great!"

The words from some unknown man, made her gasp and swing her head up to look.

"It's just Lars," Zagan whispered, but he let her see.

To the right, at the other end of the coffee table, on yet another leather armchair, slouched Lars Trask, the bass player of Purgatory. His long black hair disguised what he was doing but the snorting sound, then coughing and sneezing, made it clear he was snorting a line of some drug from the glass. Something shot across the table and rattled as it spun onto the floor.

She peered and frowned. Small. Brown. Disc-like. Not cocaine?

"What the fuck are you doing, Lars?" Zagan hitched forward to look. "What was that?"

Lars coughed again and wiped his nose. "Fuckin' supplier ran out of coke, crack, heroine, damn everything. It's..." Blearily, his finger swaying he pointed at the tiny brown thing on the floor. These're leftovers from someone's comeback tour. Found 'em in a cupboard. Brown fuckin' candy. N and N's, or something? They taste good too." He threw one in his mouth and chewed happily.

The chuckling by Zagan rocked her on his lap. Finally, Virginia remembered to blush. He would have seen what they'd been doing. She wanted to crawl under the table and hide. Although...Lars looked so out of it he might not have noticed.

Another man spoke up from the left.

She shut her eyes for a second. What next? Had they been filming a documentary while she sucked off Zagan?

But yes, there he was, Skoll Blade, leaning on a chair and grinning at them both. Short red hair, black nails, tattoos of spiders down his neck, fantastic vocalist and rhythm guitarist. Yes, he was fully compos mentis, and he'd been watching.

"Keep going, you two. Yep, it's me, the ass-fucking specialist. Mr. T. Rex told me she was one of my candidates."

"Not anymore. She's mine and we're leaving." He stood and helped Virginia to her feet, steadied her, adjusted her shirt. "You want this book?"

She nodded, having decided to ignore the asshole specialist.

"We have to get to the roof. I need a view to do this."

"Damn. I was taking notes too." Skoll made a *tsk* sound.

Zagan flipped him the bird. "You get enough women to take your own notes. Help Lars get to the hotel. I'll need you all soon. Cancel the concerts for the rest of the week."

"Week?" Lars let his mouth fall open then shut it with his hand. "We'll lose hundreds of thousands, man. Insurance won't cover this."

"No, but I will."

"Fine." Skoll shrugged.

Zagan led her into the main hall then out through an exit door. He put his hands on her waist, just above her hips and smiled. "You swallowed, didn't you? Even though I said not to."

Ooops. "Yes. It just happened. Is that bad?"

"I think you'll be okay. I can't detect any excessive radiation in you."

"You can tell that?"

He raised his hand and used his fingers to smooth away hair from her cheek. "I can. I can see all sorts of things, now that I have my powers back. You're different and I don't know why."

She nodded, turning her mouth down and placing her hand over his where he held her face. "A catholic school education does that."

"It's more than that. Much more." He shut his eyes and a chill slowly ran through her, like a ship being scanned by sonar. "I can't detect any radiation at all."

Surely that was good? "How are we getting to the roof? Ladder?" She raised her eyes. Four stories by normal building measurements? "Cause that's a looong way up."

"Ladder, no." He hugged her close. "We do it this way."

Then he took off into the air. They soared on a sweeping column of flame all the way to the roof, where he glided in to a gentle landing. After making sure she was ready, he let her step away.

She put her hand to her throat. "Fuck." She stomped out a few small fires – not easy to do with stilettos. Way to impress a lady, or scare her off, screaming and waving her arms like a psycho, which would no doubt result in her falling off this roof.

"That was..." Flustered, she shook her head. "Are you going to tell me all that power was all from one BJ? Ever heard of conservation of energy?"

"There is no logic to my demonic powers."

"Seriously? I mean, the calories in a bunch of sperm are miniscule. There's maybe one to two calories in a load? I could probably offset them by unscrewing a jar. Whereas flying up here with flames decorating our asses? I reckon that equals a few hundred gallons of fuel."

There was a long intense pause. Zagan studied her from top to toe and back again, lingering on all her sexy bits. Her nipples hardened and had a second go at sawing through her top. Maybe sassing a demon was a bad idea?

"A load?"

She scrambled to figure out what he meant, screwed up her eyes. Did he want geek language? "Ejaculate?"

"You know all that about cum?" His eyes flared deeper orange.

"Uh. Yeah?"

Zagan seemed to grow taller, darker, and a little more...loomy. She craned her neck back. Was that a word? As in, so tall she was about to need to see a chiropractor? It was now. *Loomy.*

"Tell me, my mortal lover. What else do you know about cum?"

If he stared any harder she'd have a hole drilled in her. "Um. Um. Fat content one percent? Protein, way less. People say there's heaps of vitamin C but that's false."

He drew in a deep breath and breathed out slow through his big, white teeth. "That is sooo *hot!*"

"Ahh. Okay. Fiiine." Getting weirder.

"I'm a sex demon and a woman knowing that turns me on." He yanked her closer and, with his large hand on her butt, held her in place. While he kissed her deeply, he ground his radioactive cock against her, around, up and down, around again, like a sexy X-rated merry-go-round, until she pressed back and groaned into his hungry mouth.

Asbestos or lead-lined panties might be a good buy next time she visited Walmart.

She fluttered her eyes open and struggled frantically to catch her breath. Being around Zagan was dangerous. "You really have to stop sucking all the oxygen from the air."

His grin was infectious and she smiled back.

"I shouldn't have let you do that. Karl may not be here but I do have his ring. Please. No more kissing me, or shoving your hand down my...my..."

She switched to feeling where his cock pulsed on her clit. If he unzipped himself and pushed down her tights, then wiggled aside her panties with his fingers, then slid that damn big thing into her, opening her up, slow-like.

Inferno. She had to stop thinking like that.

Had or hadn't she ever made love to Karl? She vaguely recalled *something* going into her pussy. Something big, wriggly, started with T.

Tentacle? Dangerous Bob could not be right. She was not dirty like that.

Absentmindedly, she cruised her tongue tip across her lip.

"Do that again." Zagan purred like a starved lion with a meaty bone.

She shut her mouth and pressed her lips together. "Did you hear me?"

"I heard you. You want me to stop, don't recite sex facts."

She raised one brow. That was an interesting requirement. "Okay."

"Also." He did that mind-blowing thing with his cock again, infinitesimally circling his groin against her, making her *want*. "And..."

"Mmm. Yes?" she asked, still in a fog, wanting to groan, to whimper, but holding back.

"Stop looking so fuckable. Stop being female. And absolutely don't give me ideas about sticking my cock or my tail in your pussy."

He wasn't asking much. She rolled her eyes. Brakes came on. Did he say tail? *Naaaa. Don't be silly.*

"Virginia, I really need to figure out why you do not have a trace of radioactivity showing in this delectable body despite swallowing my jizz."

"Maybe I... Fuck. Stop doing that. I'm just very..." *Swallow.* Down below, things like *probably* her pussy, were making squishy sounds. She could get a job putting out fires she was that wet. "Maybe I'm just healthy."

"I think it's more than that. However. To business." He released her. "You may watch me analyze the thaumaturgical atmosphere."

At that her brain woke her up. *Psst.* She focused – a little cross-eyed but fine. "You what?"

"You'll see."

CHAPTER 6

After nudging off his shoes, Zagan padded to the very edge of the roof and faced outward, looking across the breadth of the streetlight bejeweled city. He stripped off his shirt and stood with his arms thrust out and up, and with his fists bunched. His blood-orange flame tattoos writhed across his bare back. He roared like a barbarian king standing before his people, daring a newcomer to defeat him.

Sweat dribbled slowly down the prime A-grade muscled contours of his back, sizzling and leaving trails of steam.

Virginia's fingers twitched. *Must not touch.*

Bright cracks opened in his skin. Within them, lava seemed to flow – as eye-scalding orange as melted metal.

Eww. Must not touch because fingers would get all nasty hot and owie. Was there something wrong with having a boyfriend you could use for a toaster? Wait. Not boyfriend. Friend. Friendy friend. She straightened her top. Totally *not* sexy hot friend.

A few streets away, a fire engine's siren screamed. Red lights circled and flashed off the sides of buildings.

"We must leave before they arrive. Our burning path to the rooftop must have alerted them." Zagan splayed his fingers and began to intone some mysterious incantation. "Oom zhala kaz a min. Oom zhala..."

The gouts of fire now shooting from his fingertips wouldn't be helping calm the fire fighters either.

A car's engine started in the car park and Virginia sneaked closer to the edge.

From the open window of the car, someone shouted. "Going to

the hotel now! Had to call the Fire Department! You set the sofa on fire, man! Not good!"

"Ahh." Zagan leaned over. "Sorry!"

"Sorry isn't good enough. Insurance, dude, insurance." The car screeched in a half-circle and drove off.

"You forget I can afford it!" Zagan resumed his position, shook out his fingers. "Where was I?"

"Uh." She thought back. "Second Oom zhala?"

"Yes." As he recited the air seemed to shiver and grow tense. Her eyeballs strained as if trying to see something far, far away. A green speck appeared to the left, over the sea, from the direction of Karl's castle. It arrowed toward them, enlarged rapidly, then spun in until she could see it was the green book of her dreams. The book jetted away toward the city, leaving a trail of singing, scintillating green. Sparkling flecks fluttered down, faded, and vanished.

The quiet of the night returned, except for the dominating blare of the fire engine siren.

She stuck her fingers in her ears and yelled, praying she could lip read. "Was that the Necrosexi-texmexicon?"

"It was, but that was the book in the past. The thing has definitely gone to the Zon and we need to capture it before it implodes the entire universe. The Zon contains so many books that it could easily tip past the critical mass and become a giant black hole of books. With the Necrosexi-texmexicon there, anything might happen."

"Sounds bad," she whispered.

He nodded. "Shopping would never be the same again. We have to get going. I need men with steel sinews, hearts of gold, and big guns to venture in with us. Men who aren't afraid to die or be terribly mutilated in the name of goodness."

Big guns? Her dirty mind went off on a tangent but she whipped it back into line. "For a demon you are so damn conflicted."

"That's part of my punishment – being forced to live on Earth as a rock star billionaire, be good, and have heaps of sex but with women I can only fuck once. Sometimes the ache to do evil consumes me." Then he grabbed her, ran across the roof, and jumped off the other side of the building.

On the way down, he kissed her. "For example, doing this is pure torture." He resumed the kiss.

She wasn't quite sure she believed him, especially when he stuck his tongue in and swizzled it around. This demon had a huge tongue.

When their feet smacked into the ground, they were still kissing. Clearly, it was a longer distance down than up.

He paused. "Though maybe..." He grabbed her hair and made her arch her neck. "If I do that and then *this*." He sank what seemed to be claws into her ass.

Where the hell had those come from? Even through her tights, the sharp points drew delicious little spots of pain on her skin.

"It might be evil?" He forced another kiss onto her that made her shudder and melt right down to her toes.

When he stopped, she took a moment to recover, using her grip on his solid muscly shoulders to steady herself. *Oooh. Yum.*

She gripped him a few more times, in a few more places, not wanting to fall over accidentally. "I'm not so sure this is evil."

"You could be right. We should double check?"

"Mmm-hmm." She nodded as well as she could.

"Good thinking. Stay still. I wouldn't want to miss."

Her half-naked demon kissed her, again. She sighed at his passion. Every sexual part of her stirred and wakened. Her toes curled and the ground seemed to shake. The world faded into darkness.

Was this one of those black-outs you got gratis with super good orgasms? She didn't recall an orgasm. Minor detail.

"Zagan," she whispered. "The world's gone black."

His ardent reply was mouthed against her lips. "The floodlights are on a timer."

She peeked past his shoulder. *Oh.* "You spoiled it."

"You want black? Next time I'll bring chloroform."

"Now that *would* be evil."

"Good to know."

CHAPTER 7

After hurriedly retrieving his golden Stratocaster, dragging on his shirt, and tossing the guitar into the Zagan mobile, they set out on a roundabout route to collect the rest of the band.

The Zagan mobile had been covered in every national magazine possible but it was still a surprise to be sitting in it. Virginia smiled and caressed the padded front seat. All gold on the outside, platinum engine, powerful as a speeding lion, gleaming and smooth enough to be a butt plug, and heavy as a brick. The craft got one mile to the gallon and had to be followed by a fuel truck to get farther than the corner store.

The Monster, Zagan called it.

They picked up Lars and Skoll from the hotel. They piled into the spacious back seats. But Crush, Purgatory's drummer, had gone to a house he was helping to build on a terraced road above the ocean. They pulled up on the quiet street outside the partly erected three-story structure. Brilliant lights bathed the area.

"This is going to be an orphanage." Zagan patted her hand then slipped out and beckoned to Virginia to join him. "The man has issues. I might need a woman's touch to get him to come with us. When he was a boy, his uncle would torture him each night."

"Ohmigod. Why? What happened?" She eyed the big man. He shone in the lights and looked almost naked from a distance. As they approached, she realized he actually was naked.

"He would read books to Crush like Sleeping Beauty, and other fairy tales, over and over, when all the poor boy wanted was to play with his toy soldiers and run around the house being an airplane. Unspeakable torture."

"Uh-huh. I see." Weird, but she supposed...

Were those hammering sounds? She frowned. Her instinct was to run up and yell at him to stop. "How can he build a house naked? The construction tools. The possibility of accidents. I'm cringing."

Zagan took her hand and squeezed. "Don't worry. Crush is a hard man. Harder than anyone I know. He does it to show he's tough. After that childhood accident when the tower of building blocks fell on his head, he needs to remind himself that he has courage."

Childhood had done bad things to this man. Seriously bad.

"Don't say anything about the scars," Zagan said in a muffled aside. "He thinks he's so ugly no one will want him."

"I've seen them in pictures. Poor man."

"There's more. On the way to school one morning, he saw his mother mauled by a dog."

"Ohmigod!" Her heart was already aching for him but this was the last straw. "She was killed?"

"Her toe needed a bandage. It was a chihuahua. Big one." His mouth turned down. "Don't mention *any* of these things to his face."

That was a lot of things to be tortured by.

"I have trouble remembering shopping lists, but I'll try."

"Someday a good woman will show him he's worthy of love."

Then Crush swung around and she saw the rest of him properly. Her eyes widened. *Oh boy.*

His cock was a masterpiece of metal art. It gleamed with stainless steel. Things stuck out everywhere. The man either had a penchant for piercings or he'd already nailed his dick over and over with a nail gun. *Owie.*

He had an erection too. A big one. As an engineering feat it would rival the Eiffel Tower. Consolation prize – at least he'd not done his balls.

Crush nodded at her then grumbled. "You brought a girl to see me build?"

"Be nice, Crush, or I'll melt your dick. I need you on a mission."

His laugh surprised her and shook her eardrums. "Hehehe. I will be nice. See this one?" He lifted his cock so she could see the metal in the lights he had rigged. The one piercing he ran his finger over was an outline of a cat's face. Under it was tattooed, *Hello Pussy.*

She merely raised her eyebrows. "I see it."

"Is joke. The girls like it. Especially when I run it inside them."

Zagan tsked. "If you weren't the best drummer... One of these days we'll teach you how to talk to women, Crush."

"I don't need talk."

Virginia's schlong detector went into overdrive and it'd been sulking for hours, since the guy at the concert. "May I?" she asked Crush, indicating his cock.

He made an agreeable, yet puzzled, sound.

Gingerly she laid her hands on it. The feel was like massaging a barbed wire fence, but beneath all the stainless steel was a true schlong.

Alarm crept in when she realized Crush had stopped breathing. His eyelids quivered but otherwise he seemed fine. *Phew.* She concentrated, screwing up her face.

"What?" Crush sounded worried.

"I'm getting visions...visions of your future. You will meet a small, blonde, and pretty woman who will make you very happy as well as scream a lot." She smiled at him. "Your sperm count's good too. Keep eating that spinach."

"I don't need no future telling. Or no woman who makes *me* scream. *I* make *them* scream."

She shrugged and took away her hands. "I'm never wrong."

Without saying anything, Crush swung about and did a funny pelvic movement. The distinct bang of a hammer echoed. When he stepped away, she could see a nail that he'd driven home. Crush lifted a shirt and pants from a peg.

"That was my cock. Is why I make women scream when they come."

"Whaa?" She glanced at the nail again. He was so hard he could drive nails? Really? She pursed her lips – imagining what must happen. *Gaawwd, damn.*

As he sauntered past her toward the car, he bent and whispered in her ear. "Free trial for you."

For a second she stayed put, mouthing a swear word or two.

All that metal. She shuddered. "No fucking *way*."

Zagan shook his head. "He's a show off."

"I thought he was tortured and couldn't make love to women? And you said you needed a woman's touch to get him to come."

Author hurriedly rethinks her word choice and types faster. Nothing to see here.

"I did say that, didn't I? I think he likes you. But I never said he didn't have lovers. He goes through hookers like a receptionist goes through post-it notes. But none of them can get him to think he's worth shit." Zagan walked away.

"If he comes near me with that cock, he'll be sorry!"

What would a big fucking magnet do to those piercings?

"He won't," he yelled back. "You're mine now. He won't touch you."

Oh crap.

Karl had said those words to her. *Mine.* She remembered that. What was she doing?

But she headed after them. Time to cut loose. Let them go in and get this evil book. Stay back and sit on her hands. That was what she should do. Be a good fiancée. Stay the hell away from Zagan.

Inside her mind she could hear someone chuckling quietly.

She snapped. *What?*

Don't get snippy with me. Read the cover, Miss Virgin Captive. You ain't getting out of this book without being fucked sideways with multiple implements. Say hello to Mr. Metal Dick from me.

Smartassier by the second. She tasered her inner voice then blew away the smoke. Silence at last. It was worth losing some brain cells.

She scribbled a note to herself – get new book cover ASAP. Besides, it should really say, *almost-virgin.*

CHAPTER 8

It took two hours to make the trip into the city to the Zon. They'd had to stop to refuel the fuel truck, then again to pick up Mr. T. Rex. It had been crowded in the back with all those large men jostling for room. Strangely no one had wanted to sit on anyone else's lap.

Now here they were, across the street from the Zon. She'd heard it had grown over the years. From a single office block it had become this – a moving, rumbling monstrosity that was slowly expanding, crawling over the adjacent buildings, and eating them. The old disappeared, ground under the Zon's new outskirt rooms. The old was turned into the meat of the Zon's structure – new walls, new bricks, new whatever it decided it needed.

Virginia looked up, and up, and up.

Big. As in, the very top of this hodge-podge of a building was in the clouds. From down here it resembled a giant snail made of office bits. Smoke from crushed concrete and brick puffed into the air at the edges. The ground underfoot trembled. As if nothing unusual was happening, people filed in and out the many doors. She guessed that to them, the Zon's behavior had become commonplace.

The last of the men climbed from the gold vehicle and slammed down the butterfly-wing door. Dangerous Bob was here already.

Six men. Virginia raised an eyebrow as she surveyed them.

Zagan – man with radioactive cock. Crush – metal-pierced cock. Skoll – ass to cock fetish. Lars...he'd probably snort things with his cock. Mr. T. Rex – dino cock. And last of all, man with either the mostest or the leastest, Dangerous Bob – man with artificial cock.

There was a theme going on here. Someone clearly needed a new hobby. Though she wasn't going to say who for fear of being in the next book as the virgin captive of the gang-banging orangutans.

Bob had been digging weapons from the boot and distributing them – everything from rocket launchers to machine guns. This was so illegal. Before the Necrosexi-texmexicon entered the Zon, carrying weapons like this on Main Street would've been grounds for being locked up. Reality was already suffering. Given another week, the Canadians would be invading and holding dark rites while chanting, *winter is coming*.

"Ready?" Zagan looked them over as they nodded or said yes. Then he beckoned. "Come, Virginia."

Time to be firm. She leaned back against the Zagan mobile, patted it, smiled. "I'll stay here and mind the car. You don't need me and I don't want to get shot."

He stepped up to her then bent his head and whispered, "I do need you."

"I can't be with you," she whispered back. "I'm going to be married. Besides, you said it was dangerous around you."

"It is. I am."

She raised a skeptical eyebrow. "I can't have sex with you."

"Virginia." Zagan breathed deeply then he leaned in and planted his hands on the car to either side, caging her in. He murmured to her ear, his bristled cheek brushing hers. "You're everything to me and I never ever want to hurt you. But I'm a demon. My cum is radioactive. I'm one step away from being a creature of your worst nightmares and I'm a killer who makes evil clowns look like girl scouts with cookies."

From the corner of her eye, she could see that his irises were on fire, again. *Gulp*. Was this his spiel to make her run away fast? Because it was working.

He licked all the way around her outer ear. "And we still don't know what might happen if I come inside you."

Oh hell. She'd forgotten how to blink and he was smiling down at her from two inches away. Virginia swallowed.

"I'm a dangerous demon and my heart is pleading with me to let you go."

"Dangerous? Really? You?" Her voice squeaked. "I'd never have guessed. So, we're in agreement, you don't need me inside the Zon."

"On the other hand, my head is screaming at me to take you with me. If I need a power boost, I might have to find an alternative to fucking you."

What? Her mouth fell open. Tiny bit of a contradiction there.

"Heart." She nodded fast. "Yup. Go with that. Your head, pfft, it's got no idea."

Zagan pushed away from the car, straightened. "It's okay. Dangerous Bob agrees as long as I don't stick my cock in your pussy."

While she was still processing the reasoning in that, Dangerous Bob arrived and scooped her up. He ambled into the Zon's entryway with her over his shoulder.

Betrayal!

"Bob! How could you?" The temptation to kick and drum her hands on him came and went. If bricks didn't work on Bob, lesser force wouldn't.

Why was Bob naked from the waist up?

He muttered some choice expletives that came down to, *If we have to do this to get Karl back, then we're doing it.*

So that was his priority. Now she was annoyed as well as upside down, ass up, over his shoulder. She sighed. Seemed like she spent a part of every day like this. Maybe she should keep a book on her to read? Or, she eyed his bare skin, play tic-tac-toe? If only she had a marker pen...

They headed for a small entry to the left of the main checkpoint. By twisting her head around she could see a sign above. *Cover models for virgin captive stories.*

So this was why the naked torso. Cover model disguise.

Bob waited for an attendant to process them. A young blonde woman in a black corset and leather skirt skipped over, swishing her crop. *Prudence Prim* was on the name tag over her left breast.

At the sight of Dangerous Bob's bare chest, she stopped dead and her eyes widened.

She unfurled a long scroll and began muttering while underlining words with her crop. "Eenie meenie, miny moe. Man titties! Man titties. Ah! Directive three million and two, section nine, paragraph C. Male nipples. Hmm. Oh my."

From a drawer beside the entry she drew something then tapped Bob's chest in time with her words. "Naughty, naughty boy! No naked man nips in the Zon. Put these pasties on those nipples ASAP!"

She watched eagerly, with her tongue tip on her lip, while Bob planted a pair of bright pink pasties on his chest.

Virginia giggled. Even Bob's back was going red. The poor man was embarrassed.

Once they were through the cover model entry, he deposited her on her feet. She adjusted her tights and T-shirt, glared at him, but stayed put. From the other side of the barrier, five men grinned at her and Dangerous Bob's decorated nipples.

"Grrr." If any man could master an animal growl it was Bob. He flipped the tassels on the pasties so they spun, as if daring them to make fun of him.

Did she dare? The consequences of taunting Bob could be hazardous but his recent betrayal niggled her.

From the corner of her mouth, she muttered, "You're rockin' those." When he shot her a suspicious look, she waggled her eyebrows. "Serious strippergram material, man."

He growled again.

She turned away before grinning. *Score!*

A big open door frame affair, that was obviously detecting metal, formed the checkpoint for the average visitor. She guessed Bob had been worried about his artificial cock being detected and ruled inadmissible.

As if passing on some secret, Zagan gathered the other men in a circle and whispered at them, then they all stripped off their shirts.

As they passed through the checkpoint, they were each handed pasties to wear. They stuck them on their nipples and gave Bob a thumbs-up signal. He shook his head but smiled.

Now there were six half-naked men with pasties on their nips. Oh my, all her Christmases had come at once.

Their weapons were being banned though. A pile of their guns built at the checkpoint.

Zagan wandered over and joined her and Bob. He shrugged. "They don't sell them in here so we can't bring them in. The Necrosexi-texmexicon is going to be hard to take down."

Bob grumbled in his sweary way. *We'll find new ones. A place this big, there'll be something.*

Suddenly, girly screaming broke out. The shrill noise ricocheted around the large foyer and Virginia cringed. A horde of women, both young and old, burst in and swarmed toward the checkpoint. They pointed at Zagan and blew kisses. He grinned and waved back.

"It's Purgatory!" shrieked some. "It's Zagan!" screamed others. Yet another squealed, "I wanna fuck him until my pussy's on fire."

"Man, she's a hot chick too." Zagan scratched his chin.

Virginia kicked his ankle and glared at the demon. An urge to say *mine* to him hit her and almost passed her lips. She pulled herself up sharply.

"What?" Zagan seemed nonplussed.

"Nothing. Just if Dangerous Bob does any more swearing, between him and you, this place will explode from an overdose of crazy girls and screaming."

Luckily the girls were being kept on the other side.

The men were all through except for Crush and he was held up because Prudence wasn't sure about his mostly metal cock. Bob had been right to take the alternative entry.

Prudence tilted her head and loudly sucked her purple lipsticked lips. She'd made Crush unzip and place the offending member on the counter. Currently, she was prodding it with her crop and pouting.

Virginia couldn't tell if Crush was happy, mad, or intrigued by her attention.

"I don't knowww. Are you sure it's all yours? It looks wrong and I can't find it in the instructions scroll."

Crush muttered something to her.

She clapped her hands. "What a good idea."

He put it away and zipped up.

Tongue out to concentrate, she slowly wrote something on her scroll.

"There! I've filed it under roosters. Just keep it in your pants when you're in the book sections. Sex toys area, you can let it allll hang out." Her voice went into husky tone territory, only there weren't no sled dogs to be seen for miles. "Nipple clamps, floggers, cock pumps, vibrators – we got them all." Prudence winked.

As he sauntered through, she gave him a smack on the ass with the crop then whispered, "Meet me after work by the Hall of Dildos."

The small twerk Crush did was enough to make a girl roll her eyes.

Multiple doors led away from the foyer but Zagan stopped them under the big one labelled *Books*.

"This is it. Further down it divides into electronic or print books. I think print is where the Necrosexi-texmexicon will be, but we'll have to split up." He glanced at them. "With me is Dangerous Bob, Crush, and of course you, Virginia. Lars, Skoll, and Mr. T. Rex, you send me a text message if you find it. Okay?"

They nodded.

He shook their hands. "May we all survive this terribly hazardous mission without getting hurt. Good luck, and if the worst happens and you die, I'll put in a word for you with the big man downstairs."

Lars and Skoll went pale. Mr. T. simply chuckled.

Out of the corner of her mouth, Virginia whispered. "Next time, let me write the speeches."

"Sure," he whispered back. "As long as you're naked and in my bed while we write it."

"Stop that! You're dangerous, remember? Why are you so fixated on sex?"

"Because *A*. I'm a sex demon. *B*. I can't help it. I'm a junkie and you're my favorite drug."

She shook her head and set off down the white hall toward the next signs. "I'm not sure I want to be a compared to heroin."

"It's a compliment. Romantic! Like...like, saying when I'm away from you there's nothing I crave more than to be with you. When I'm with you my world *is* you. I want to hug you and kiss you, make love to you until you holler my name. Sometimes I want you so much I can't breathe."

She stopped to look. He was down on one knee and had his hand planted over his heart. "So now I give you an asthmatic attack? Damn." She trudged on. "Let me write the speeches!"

"You can't write the lovey dovey ones!"

Crap. He had a point.

He got in a last word. "And stop twitching that fucking sexy ass when you walk away."

Don't make a rude gesture. Don't. But when else in her life would she get to insult a demon? She flipped him the bird. She'd just have to have a sick bag on hand when he tried his next lot of romantic lines on her.

CHAPTER 9

The hallways for books were endless. Doorway illustrations gave hints as to what would be inside. Heaving bosoms, ballroom dresses, and kilts were on the historical romance door. Once through that doorway, there was yet another corridor and more doors leading to more subgenres like highlanders and regency. The science fiction doorway showed lasers and aliens. They went down corridor after corridor, opening doors, alert for anything odd, trying to appear like normal curious shoppers in the crowd toddling through the Zon.

After yet another fruitless search, Zagan held up his hand. "This is getting us nowhere. I've seen nothing that suggests a book that can alter reality has been through here."

He drew out his cell phone and texted three times. Then he lowered the phone.

Nothing? Dangerous Bob cocked his head.

"No. They're not answering. I figure we have three choices. Blunder about trying to find them, or we can stay here, still with no clue, or I can enhance my power and see what I can detect." He turned and studied Virginia, swung his gold guitar off his back and propped it against the wall.

Oh-oh. She took a step away and hit a door. Cornered. *What an unexpected development. Not.*

"Good choice," Zagan murmured. "Contemporary urban fantasy." Then he was on her, taking her wrists in his grasp and pinning them above her head with one hand.

Fuck. She didn't like this, did she? Being grabbed by a vibrant, shirtless, male demon who she knew wanted to have his dirty, smutty way with her?

Even if her panties were damper than a swamp full of alligators in monsoon season, she was still outraged. As a woman with a valid virgin card, she would protest vigorously.

The yawn in the back of her mind warned her. *Protest? You mean like this? Oh no! Save me, save me!*

The tasering effect hadn't lasted long enough. Her conscience cross sneering-inner-onlooker had returned.

Sneering? That hurt me, sweetums. P.S Monsoons are in India. Alligators are not.

Ignoring it seemed the best choice when her priority needed to be getting loose and running.

"Where do I bite you first?" Zagan smiled as he looked her over. "Neck?" He moved closer until his body mass pinned her too.

A little wriggle of her pelvis assured her that she was fastened there well and truly. It also told her his cock was well and truly hard. Thoughts of escaping went bye byes. She whimpered.

"Can't get away? Hmm? Poor girl."

He bit the side of her neck. His teeth sank in, hurting her, but in a nice way that sent throbs through her muscle. So deliciously primal. Her gasp seemed to amuse him.

She was going to lose her virgin card.

"You mustn't do this!"

"Mustn't I?"

Dangerous Bob had developed an acute interest in a door that went to war stories. Crush was watching them avidly, as if this was better than any TV channel he'd ever seen.

She showed her teeth to both him and Zagan.

"The kitty cat snarls?" Zagan kicked the door open and hustled her through backward. The door clicked shut and they were alone. "Let's see if I can be your urban fantasy."

"Wait, wait." The determination in his gaze was both daunting and exhilarating. Her heart was already doing a tango on fast forward.

He'd let go of her wrists but she figured she'd not get far if she ran. Plus she'd likely trip, sprain an ankle, sprawl on her face...then he'd pounce on her, wrench down her tights, worm his hand between her legs and a finger up inside, she'd be sooo wet, and tight...she'd squeal, then come enough times to make a porn star jealous... She sighed and cleared her throat.

From the back of her mind came heavy breathing.

Well, that was a first. Her inner voice was speechless.

She couldn't help checking her demon out. The pasties had disappeared in a puff of flame and smoke. The fiery pattern on his bare chest had gone into intense burn and churn mode – enough that she wondered if he'd feel hot if she ran a finger around those nipples, or a tongue.

Zagan had a distinctive aroma that struck her whenever she breathed in this close to him. She took another sniff. Yes. Brimstone and magic with a hint of down and dirty sex, like he'd accidentally put a condom in the toaster.

She shook her head.

"I never said yes...to whatever you have in mind."

"True. But I'm about to coerce a yes from those sweet, luscious lips." This time after he held her against the wall, he bit the upper swell of her breast.

"Zagan!" Her knees wobblified, a condition that really should be in the medical journals.

"First, this comes off." He grabbed the sides of her T-shirt and quickly stripped it off over her head.

She covered her breasts.

"Now we're both a little naked." He whistled and pulled her hands away. "Let me see. Nice tits. Nice lacy red bra. Love your color scheme. Red's my favorite too."

"*That* is your chat up romance line?"

"Do I need one?" He spun her so she faced the wall and molded himself to her, trapping her again.

"Yes, you do," she managed to squeak.

There was no way she could get free. With each heartbeat, the heat from his body throbbed deeper into her. Something stiff pressed between her butt cheeks. She swore she could hear his cock. *Throb, throb.*

Psychiatric help required STAT.

"Karl needs us to do this, Virginia."

She sucked in a shuddery breath.

Ohmigod. Something was slithering up her side. If this was a part of Zagan, it wasn't his cock, not unless it was detachable and operated by remote control.

"I want to be inside you so bad. My cock in you, my cum in you. My name on your pretty lips. I want to be so close to you no one will be able to tell where one of us ends and the other begins."

She thought that through. "As in smooshed together like amoebas do it?"

"You could put it that way."

"Sort of Vulcan mind meld plus superglue?"

"Kinky. I like where this is heading."

"If we need surgery afterward to get us apart, it's a no."

With his fingers raked into her hair, he dragged her head around. "You do know you don't have a choice?"

The slithery thing nudged at her tights as if looking for the way in. She wiggled her butt and tried to deter it. "Zagan!"

"Yes?"

"Do I need bug spray? There's something poking at me down there." His chuckle made her bristle. "What?"

"That's my tail, dear girl. I've decided since I can't come inside your cunt, I'll fuck you with my tail."

Tail? She thought fast. He was a demon. *Tail, tail, tail.* All she could think of was cartoons. "Is it red with a barb at the end?"

"Close. Not wanting to scare you, but it's alive with fire, like my markings." That baritone voice and what he meant to do to her, made her pussy moisten and her nipples bunch up like pencil rubbers aiming to erase graffiti from the wall.

Her nose was getting squashed. She turned her head, breathing heavily through parted lips and finding she had a nice appreciation for the way he'd caught her between a hard demon and a hard wall.

Zagan kissed her full on the mouth. His tongue slipped in at the same time his tail gave up on pulling down her tights and slid between her legs. She gasped. It prodded harder. Cloth ripped and without further ado, it rammed determinedly up inside her. Thick. Thicker than she'd thought it was. The ridges of the barb tormented her as the tail squirmed into her pussy, driving a tunnel through her slickness. Pleasure ripped through her.

She thrust her ass back at him but her thighs shook so much that she sagged a little down the wall.

"Oh yeah. I can feel that. So fucking good." The rasp of his words said he was loving this too. "You know what? I can taste every molecule of you with my tail, and it tells me you've got zero residue from my cum. So I think it's safe to do this too."

"Do whut?" Her brain had fuzzed out, what with his tail invading her most intimate place.

Her tights ripped again and, shocking her awake, his fingers probed her other hole. One sank slowly in past the tightness, relaxing her slowly.

She groaned.

He's going to fuck both your holes. Her inner voice giggled. *Go, go, go.*

There was something infinitely pervy about an inner voice that wanted to watch.

"I can't stop myself, baby. Hang on for the ride. I can tell from the responses of your little hole that you've done this before."

Her eyes widened. She had? She'd done anal? And she'd forgotten? Whoever arranged her amnesia was in deep trouble. "I did?"

"Yeah, you did. And you will."

Then his cock was probing at her too, dead center on that forbidden entrance, which apparently wasn't as forbidden as she recalled.

"More," he croaked. His cock, as hot as could be without frying her, and his devilish tail, both forged inward.

"Wait, wait." Desperate, not thinking too well, she burbled out. "Isn't lube needed for *that*? I mean, I heard it was." She panted some more, whining, he wasn't stopping, not yet. "And aren't you too big for *there*?"

He laughed. "*That* and *there*? I'm just right. You can take it. Lube is for humans." As his teeth fastened on her nape, his hand smoothed its way down her belly, all the way to clit territory.

What with the double fucking of her pussy and ass going on, and now her clit getting a gentle massage with the V of his fingers, and the tip of them, and now those fingers were circling, and pressing, and *unngh*.

She lost track of thoughts and presented her ass outward so she could get more of him in her.

"That's it. Take me. Take all of me. I don't need lube, Virginia, because I have natural lube."

"Convenient," she gurgled. When she fluttered her eyes open he was watching her intently.

"Being a sex demon has advantages. Who needs lube when you

have lava?"

"What? Lava? You're not really –" She found her mouth taken by his in a possessive, silencing kiss.

Fuck. What this demon could do with his tail. As the rhythm of sex took them both, his tail surged back and forth, fucking her in spirals, in tandem with his enormous hot cock, even in corkscrew, as if she was a tight bottle needing to be plugged. Her moisture dripped out when his tail withdrew, along with whatever demon juice he'd taken her ass with. The rear and inner thighs of her tights dampened as the wetness dribbled down her. Her mouth was open but she'd forgotten how to kiss him despite him fucking her there too with his long tongue.

She was drowning in sex. The sounds of him slapping into her. The wet noises. The pain of his bites and hair pulling. The sting when his tail or cock was too rough. The primitive smell of mating. Her mind shut down. Fucking didn't need it.

Pleasure rose, humming through her from where he shoved himself into her, widening her, making her body into his sex toy. She panted, moaned, and even squeaked her way to the edge of a climax. Her body ached for that last, exquisite surge. That push. The need was *there*, pulsing, filling her.

"Come for me," he told her at precisely the right moment.

Wasn't any stopping it. With her lips parted and her eyes sightless, she came, arching, crying out his name. The orgasm blasted away all coherent thought.

Zagan kept thrusting into her, a relentless machine ridden by the directives of sex. Tail and cock, in and out, fucking her, until he too cried out his release. His cum pumped inside her, hotter than hell, triggering another wave of pleasure.

She was his, totally and thoroughly fucked.

He hugged her to him as they panted their way back to reality.

"Let me go." She licked drool from her lips.

"Why? Your legs are shaking. You'll slide down the wall."

"Maybe I wanna clean it."

But he released her and she turned around. *Wow*. Zagan looked even sexier with his pants down around his ankles and his cock glistening with her moisture and his cum. But one other thing drew her gaze – a set of black, glossy horns curled from his head.

"You've got something new on your head."

"These?" He reached up and ran his hand along one horn. "It's because of you. With all this power, I can't hide my true self anymore."

"I love them." She looked him up and down again. Why was this so attractive? "I'm such a dirty girl."

"Oh, you are. You are." He grinned back at her and hauled up his pants, zipped up.

"How can I walk around here now? I've got holes in my tights and cum on me."

These small things never did bother the average romance character. Why her?

"I can fix that." He bent and stripped off her tights and panties then wiped between her legs while kissing her like he wanted to remember her taste until the end of time.

When he was done, she was sure her eyes were glazed and she'd lost a few brain cells.

Dayum. "Stop cheating. Kissing me isn't a substitute for explaining why I won't dribble cum as I walk."

He shook his finger at her. "Naughty. Dirty mouth. You won't because I say you won't. I'm a sex demon and such knowledge comes with the title. But you will have to keep your T-shirt down if you don't want to show off your hot little sex-reddened pussy."

Gah. She yanked down the edges. "Give me my tights. It's better than this."

"Can't."

"Why?"

"I ate them."

Her mouth fell open but no words would come.

Was he telling the truth? Was it possible? He was a demon. They weren't on the floor. He'd eaten them? Really?

"You didn't?"

"They tasted good too." He winked and slowly checked her out, especially where her T-shirt ended. "Besides, I wanted you like this, without panties."

Glaring at him seemed the best thing option.

Important: remember to never ask him to do the laundry. Or look after her cat.

CHAPTER 10

Zagan beckoned to the three of them. The ebook section door ahead was blasted off its hinges and smoking.

"We have to be on the alert from now on! My power tells me the Necrosexi-texmexicon is definitely down there! But I still can't get hold of Lars, Skoll, or Mr. T. Something has gone wrong," he yelled, very loudly, signaling the next plot development in as obvious a way as possible.

Virginia took her hands off her ears and frowned. "We still have no weapons."

He rapped the gold guitar hanging at his back. "I have this."

"Does it shoot bullets or ninja stars or explode?"

"It squashes things when I hit them with it."

"Uh-huh."

Dangerous Bob gave it the once over then materialized a piece of four by two from somewhere unknown.

Shit. Virginia blinked. So that's where it came from.

The last of their squad, Crush, just patted his groin and chuckled.

The man was so up himself, if tortured. What could he do with that?

"Good." Zagan nodded. "We're all armed then, except Virginia, and she doesn't count because she's a girl."

Ohmigod. She was going to have to do a lot of ignoring today, or she was going to kill somebody whose name started with Z. "The demon loses ten points on the marriageable scale. *I* have my razor sharp wit."

Zagan smiled. "I know you do. I'm counting on it."

"And gains fifteen on the rebound."

Crush chuckled while also managing to leer at her almost exposed bottom.

For the fiftieth time she tugged the shirt down. If they had to crawl through any ceiling ducts on this book finding expedition, she was going last.

"Remember, eyes peeled for abnormalities that might mean the book's been here. When we catch it, we have to make it open a portal so Karl and the Sea Wolves can return here, then send it through, back to wherever it came from."

They sneaked through the door and continued on past many askew doors. There'd been bad things happening. Debris and actual paper pages littered the floor. People ran past them toward the exit, screaming, with panic written on their faces...in big letters.

"Why the paper, Zagan?" She stopped at his shoulder and peered through the nearest genre door – Erotic Literature.

"I think the Necrosexi-texmexicon is making the electronic contents of the stories become real. This is where the worst of it seems to be, and I can sense the book too." He checked his guitar, like a ninja checking his sword, putting his hand to the neck where it jutted above his shoulder.

They filed through the beaten-up door and were faced with another long corridor, immensely long, that disappeared into a haze in the distance. It was deserted and there were thousands more doors to either side.

"Be very careful," he added. "Stick close to me."

Good advice but where would a story be if no one did anything stupid?

"Sure." She couldn't get over seeing those horns sticking out of his head.

What would it be like to hold them while he made love to her? Preoccupied, she wandered over to a door labelled Disasters in Book Covers and wrenched it open, found yet another corridor of doors, each one covered with a different book cover. The place was a maze of doors. She figured these would be the stories you could buy. She checked the nearest, then screamed.

Dangerous Bob sprinted over, swearing a dirty streak. *What?*

"*It* has been here. Something awful has happened. Look." She had one hand plastered over her eyes but she peeked through her fingers.

Screechy horror violin-type music assaulted their ears for a few tense seconds.

Before them loomed a cover with a man's bare chest above a landscape of three upright dildos, a dinosaur, and an elegant woman with bright red lipstick. *Dongzilla in Mantitty City by Wetly Comeson* was proclaimed in searing white letters.

"God. It's horrible," she managed to croak out.

Bob was struck dumb. When Crush walked up and looked, all he did was squeak.

"What...has happened here?" Staggering a little, she wandered further along, and found a book cover door with a woman dressed as a short-skirted schoolgirl under the title, *fuck being subtle by Spanky Schoolgirl*. Then there was *Private Trumpet by Racy McDacy* with a woman being sexually molested by a trumpet.

"Oh my god," she whispered. "I need therapy."

Before she could go further along, Zagan called them back.

"Out! There's nothing we can do. Some things are beyond even my powers. Our Necrosexi-texmexicon book hasn't been here. These are just victims of an author with a poor taste and the ability to ass-fuck a book design program."

She was the last out and she leaned back against the Disasters in Book Covers door, breathing deeply, regaining her sanity. Close call.

From the way Crush was still quivering he was just as badly affected. Poor Bob, his eyes were wide and his eyebrows seemed permanently glued in the upright and startled position.

Focus. "If we'd opened one, what's behind the door?"

Her demon mused a second. "Just the story, I think. Though with reality being distorted, it might be dangerous to go too far in. You could be trapped in there. But come with me, all of you. There's something I need to show you."

When they returned to the main corridor he led them down to another door. The worried expression Zagan wore made her wonder what was wrong.

"I've found Skoll and Lars. It's not pretty. But this is what you have to be wary of. We must never let our attention wander."

At a door called *Hearts at War*, bearing a cover with a passionate couple kissing in a jungle, he inhaled then pulled it open. "Let's see if we can rescue them."

Whatever she'd been expecting, it wasn't this. A whole different world was before her. Miles and miles of land. Below was jungle and beyond that seemed to be crops or fields. They descended a narrow grassy path to the jungle. Grass rustled and something calf-high waddled from the bushes.

"Books!" She gasped, pointing vigorously. "Walking books!" She bent at the knees to see under them. Little legs? How cute. When had this turned into a fairy tale?

Though Crush tried to pick one up, the little books scampered away and ended up in a small herd of five or six around Virginia's ankles, bumping into her, rattling their pages, and whispering.

"They like you." Zagan grinned. "Another example of the world going weird. The Book must be close. Let's go."

The path wove between huge rainforest trees that stretched their branches overhead. The light dimmed. Sounds of squeaking apes came from the left, somewhere off the path. Virginia ducked under vines to follow Zagan. The screeching ape noises grew louder. In the gloom, figures scampered and leaped. Her heart knocked at her chest, in a distinct effort to vacate the premises.

What was going on here?

When he halted, they stopped behind him then spread out. She stood to his left.

"Damn." Zagan swore quietly. "Too late. It's Skoll. Best if you don't look. Let's go."

But even though he tried to block her view as he turned, she could see past him. A whole herd of some sort of ape was cavorting, and...having sex? Lars was in there? Somewhere? It was a boiling cauldron of apes on crack.

"Don't look." Zagan shepherded her backward.

"Why? What's he doing?"

"The Book must have got to him. Skoll always did like anal and well, now he's got it in abundance. Only I'm not sure who is doing what to who. It's a maelstrom of gangbang monkey sex."

Gulp. Saying that in one sentence had to be some sort of record.

But as she turned to leave, a thought struck. "Wait. Are those...let me guess, orangutans?"

"You know your apes. What does it matter?"

Crap. "Never mind."

An orangutan gang-bang. She'd been right not to piss off the author. Poor, poor man, What had Skoll ever done except be a filthy-minded rock musician with a liking for fucking ass?

Bitch author. Oops. Think pretty thoughts, think pretty, non-incriminating thoughts.

In a gentle and perhaps kindly reassurance, Crush squeezed Zagan's shoulder. "He's in his happy place."

If that was happy, she'd take a prison sentence with a bunch of drop-the-soap-in-the-shower sex mad crims.

Zagan trudged on. "We go through the jungle, out the other side. I know Lars is here. I can feel him. And look. That's his."

A white extension cord lay on the ground and went on as far as she could see, one cord after another, each plugged into the next.

"Why? Where'd that come from?"

"Lars always likes to stock up on those. Half the hotels we stay at, he's got to fling the TV out the window with it still on. It's a dare. An accomplishment. Especially if the TV is still on when it hits the water."

"So this is the rock musician's version of a paper trail?"

"Yes."

Once they emerged from the jungle, they found a field of red flowers that stretched from side to side and off toward the horizon. The air was hot, sticky, and stifling. The sun scorched the sky a pale blue and the path they now walked upon was gravel. Since Virginia had thrown away her stilettos long ago, she had to do a hop, skip, and *fucking ouch* dance, every now and then. Overhead, a squadron of buzzing, small planes wove in and out of each other's flight paths, attempting to shoot each other from the sky. Machine guns rattled. Bullets were no doubt perforating things. It was a war, all right, though with no romantic kissing in sight.

"Where's Lars?" All she could see was the endless sea of flowers. Then a scream of glee erupted and a patch of flowers swayed as if something was brushing them.

Dangerous Bob pointed at the moving flowers. "Fuckin' fucker."

"Yup." He was right. Lars rolled into view, squashing the edge of the flower field. On his face was ecstasy. His tongue lolled and he called out nonsense words.

"Poppies. It's a poppy field." Zagan swore along with Bob. "Let's drag him out of there, but he'll be useless for hours. The man looks like he's been chewing on the poppies."

"Gagagaga!" Lars waved and slumped again. He grabbed a bunch of flowers and stems and stuffed them in his mouth.

Two of the team out of action already. Mr. T. was still missing.

"Ow!" The little books had followed them through the jungle and one of them had nipped her ankle. She frowned, backing away but finding they wanted to huddle near her again. Had they gone feral?

When she stopped retreating, they swarmed closer to her legs, and they seemed to be shivering.

She looked up at the jungle. Something was coming from there, something that scared them.

There was a noise. Rustling. Thumping. The bushes swayed. A tree toppled with a crunch then a thud as it hit the ground.

Mr. T. burst out, yelling, and waving his short arms.

Tearing out after him came a green and obviously magical book about six feet high. Trees and grass around it burst into rainbow flame. Pages of books were spat out, spinning, by the Necrosexitexmexicon, like razor sharp Frisbees.

She felt herself pale and her fingers grow cold.

Paper cuts were the worst.

Little booklings ran past it squeaking, most of them homing in on her. Did they think she was their momma or something?

Dangerous Bob materialized his four by two.

Zagan unslung his guitar.

Guitar music twanged through the air as if announcing to the audience that a Mexican desperado had been flushed into the open, his guns firing, his mustache twirling.

Crush...she wasn't sure what he was doing but it looked rude.

The world exploded, metaphorically speaking.

Virginia stood there quaking as everyone ran at everyone else, shouting, swinging their weapons or their cocks. Or in Mr. T's case, transforming before her very wide eyes, into a Tyrannosaurus rex with big teeth and stompy feet. She scurried backward, herding the panicking booklings.

"Stay there," yelled Zagan as he stormed past. "You can't do anything."

Good to know, considering she was so scared her knees were knocking. So she sat down in the poppy field beside Lars and took up weaving.

The bangs, roars, and whistles, the planes zooming past at breakneck speed, ten feet above ground level, the crunches of bones and splatter of blood, it all said *War*, with a big *W*.

Knit one. Pearl One. Knitters said that didn't they? It was like a calming mantra.

Besides, shielding the booklings and Lars seemed the best she could do.

A hundred yards to the left, she was aware of the battle slowly rolling past. There were more screams. She peeked. Zagan was alive. The blood and other icky things flying about made her go back to weaving, after she'd soothed and patted a small, shaking book. By the time the noise abated, she'd woven a poppy stem skirt.

She rose, dragged on the somewhat holey and crooked skirt then took a breath. She looked past the smoking wreckage of a plane, past a few slumped bodies, and beyond a burnt-out tank with several steel pages jutting from its turret.

Far in the distance, Mr. T., in his gigantic T. rex form, was chewing on the Necrosexi-texmexicon. Sparks sprayed from his mouth. The book wriggled loose from his jaws and shot away. It bashed a hole in a wall that hadn't been there before, but was apparently the boundary of this story's setting, and vanished. Mr. T. lumbered after it, smashing an even bigger tear in the wall as he exited.

"Well. This is interesting. And can't be real." She rubbed her eyes.

But Zagan was nearby and had been watching the distant battle. Alongside him stood Crush and Bob. He pointed to the other side of the field, a mile or more away, where there was a purple flickering dome of electricity. From the purple dome walked forth a man. She knew him in an instant. Karl.

Karl Thulhu.

And she remembered *everything*. He was a possessive man cross tentacle monster. She distinctly recalled a long, detailed statement that ended with him saying mine, over and over, even if he hadn't wanted her china animal collection.

Oh my.

Awkward.

"The Necrosexi-texmexicon did it!" Zagan yelled to her. "It's made the portal and Karl is back. You stay there. I'll go meet him and explain everything."

Her knees wobblified again and she had to kneel among the poppies – that or fall over. Not good. Maybe this was all a dream? An opium dream? One could hope. Either that or she was going to have to explain to Karl how she'd had sex with a demon.

How was she going to choose between these two lovers? They both had places in her heart and, she supposed, elsewhere, considering where all those tentacles and that tail had been.

She didn't even have a coin on her to flip.

Decisions, decisions.

CHAPTER 11

"Okay, here we are. To the left is your typical battle scene. Do try not to step on the innards or you'll have to wash your feet when we leave." Prudence Prim had arrived with what looked like a baby dwarf hippo trotting at her heels.

Virginia squinted as they waltzed from the jungle with Prudence pointing out things of note like dead people and sizzling left-over rockets. What were they up to? The little group of tourists, mostly men, were happily taking pictures of everything from pools of blood to what looked suspiciously like a dead bookling hanging from a tree branch. She growled, wanting to smack the guy in the head.

"It's you!" Prudence said brightly as she wandered over. The little hippo squealed as it hurried to keep up. "Oh dear, whatever are you wearing?" She waggled a ruler in Virginia's direction. "Is that skin? You can't do that, dear. Not here, in a story, that's like, being seen by the general public."

What? There were dead people, or something...Virginia wasn't sure what as she hadn't looked closely...only two yards behind Prudence. The woman had even stepped over a puddle of blood to get here.

"*You* brought them. And it *is* an erotic story."

"Doesn't matter. It's a brand new rule. Like one-second new. Look, I'll check with administration." Then she bent down and whispered to the hippo. The critter snuffled into her ear and she nodded, plainly believing it was saying something. She straightened. "There. Told you it was a rule."

Hell. Was this for real? If the attendants could make up the rules like this, she was about to be shafted.

Without asking, Prudence poked at the skirt.

"Ahem." Virginia scowled and edged backward. Invasion of privacy, or what? "Aren't you supposed to be shepherding those people?"

"They're all having fun. And being law-abiding. But you....ooooh. That skirt is just on the edge of disgraceful. I may have to cite you. You simply cannot expose that much skin. Do you even have panties on?"

She folded her arms, prepared to stand her ground and wedge a book up Prudence's hoohah if she did one more poke. "Maybe. Maybe not."

"The horror!" She shuddered. "You must be joking?"

Crush sneaked up behind her and tapped Prudence's shoulder. She spun around.

"You! Darling man. Have you been a good boy?"

Though he blushed, Crush nodded.

He wasn't saying much, but at least he'd distracted Prudence from her puritanical invasion of Virginia's poppy stem skirt.

The scars on his face looked pale, as the rest of his face was so beetroot red. Prudence caressed them with her ruler. "I like these. Makes you such a beautiful man." She lowered her voice. "I wanna take you somewhere and do bad things to you. Would you let me? Hmm."

There was a pause so pregnant a herd of wildebeest popped into being in the fields and proceeded to have baby wildebeests. Virginia cocked one eyebrow. Whatever *were* wildebeests anyway?

Crush nodded shyly but croaked. "Yes, ma'am."

Wait. What? Virginia took a step and tapped Prudence on the shoulder. "You can't take him anywhere. We need him to defeat the Necrosexi-texmexicon."

"Ummm. Really? Though I know that book. It threatens the existence of the Zon itself. That's what this battle was about?"

She nodded but rummaged through her expressions and summoned a glare. "You can't have Crush. Even if I have zero idea as to what exactly he did in the battle. I mean a cock that could hammer nails is interesting and all, but does it have any other use? Seriously?"

After choking for a few seconds, Prudence recovered. "Yes," she squeaked. "I do believe so. I will do you a deal. Crush comes with me. I won't prosecute your see-through skirtness disaster."

Virginia glared harder.

"And...if you come with us, I will give you a weapon of inestimable value. The weapon to end all weapons. And probably the Necrosexi-texmexicon too. The Wand."

"The wand? What. The Fuck?" I can't go traipsing off to get this. Zagan and Karl..." Oh god, explaining time soon. "They expect me to be here."

"Pfft." Prudence hooked a finger under Crush's chin. "I have like a scifi teleport thing. You can be gone and back again in the buzz of a futuristic *zzzap* before they notice you missing. Come."

"Come? N –"

The world blinked out, went *pinnng*. And she was there. Somewhere else. Virginia looked around. There were shelves everywhere and there were dildos, and topless women with clampy things on their nipples, and others wearing dildos like cocks, and *ohmigod* it was too much. She stared at Prudence and totally nowhere else. Was this the Hall of Dildos?

"You wanted to sue me over my skirt and there's all this!" She gestured wildly without actually looking at anyone or anything. So what if she'd had tentacle sex, and tail sex, and all that. This was rude!

But Prudence merely sauntered to a display of what seemed black dog collars and steel chain leashes, then sauntered back and buckled the collar onto Crush without doing more permission wise than looking deeply into his eyes while she did so.

The little hippo squatted nearby watching everything.

God damn. Maybe Crush had found his woman? She shook her head, Concentrate on the task at hand.

"You said you had a magic wand? Who in this day and age has wands?"

"Fairy godmothers."

She'd said it so seriously that Virginia was stunned. "You're joking." She surveyed the blonde woman from heels to corset and back. "You? A fairy godmother?"

"Meh." She shrugged. "Who knows? I go with the flow. But look...I do have a wand. Here." She went to another shelf and selected something vaguely ice-cream-cone shaped but bigger. Then she returned and solemnly held up the thing.

"What? This is it?"

"It is. Behold." With a grand gesture, and a bow, Prudence presented the device to Virginia like a prize in a game show. "The Wand of Magic."

"Mmm. I don't know if this is a fair swap. It looks electrical. Where am I going to find a wall plug?"

"How the fuck do I know? Begone!"

And with that, she was back at the battle scene, and a few feet from a very unhappy looking Karl and a grinning Zagan, her demon with those sexy, black horns. Virginia blinked and tried not to fall over.

"Where have you been?" Karl's black suit looked perfect, as if he'd just returned from a wedding.

"Getting this. A, ummm, magic wand?" She held it up, waggled it.

"That's a vibrator."

"Oh shit. That bitch."

"Don't worry. I can find something to do with it." Zagan winked at her. "But now, let's go track down the Book. Where's Crush?"

Oops. "I think I just let a dominatrix with a thing for dildos get hold of him."

Zagan sniggered. "He's well and truly fucked then. We'll just have to do this without him. The Book has tried to distract us by returning Karl. But if we let it go, it will destroy this place. However." He raised his brows. "I have an idea or two. And they all involve you."

From his smug look, his ideas probably involved Zagan's favorite occupation – sex.

"Na-uh."

"Yup."

"I agree." Karl nodded solemnly. "And so will you."

Fuckitty. She pouted and tried to look disgruntled. "What do you mean, exactly?"

"You want details?" Zagan shook his head. "I'm not good at talking. Doing is more my scene." He glanced at Karl. "Let's show her how to *do*?"

"Agreed."

Oh my. Just one under-the eyebrows-stare from Karl and she had an urge to run. Those black irises... *Gulp.* Except her non-existent panties had just become sizzling, fireball hot. Which really was damn uncomfy. She *squeeezed* her thighs together and whimpered.

CHAPTER 12

"We're fucking with your head, Virginia." Karl smiled, though with his mouth only. His eyes were stone.

Scary man. Granite? Onyx? She had this urge to go up and tap on his eyeballs to check.

He continued. "We had a look through the tear in this world that the Necrosexi-texmexicon made and we have a plan for destroying the Book."

"No crazy sex?"

"No." He shook his head.

Phew. Relief. She put her hand over her heart. "You're both bastards."

"Shall we turn her over our knees and spank her for that?" Zagan flexed his hands. His horns loomed above, making him look scrumptiously intimidating.

Crap. She scurried to elaborate. "But nice bastards. Absolutely, really nice...bastards." Being around these two was like setting up house in a minefield. Which was close to the truth. She looked at the carnage, spotted a bookling trotting about with a finger in its mouth. At her frown, it froze then slowly dropped the finger.

"Later, I will spank her." Karl's mouth twitched. "We've seen where the book is. I believe it created the portal because a dinosaur was chewing on it, because it was stressed. We're going to annoy it again, get the Sea Wolves back, and then we will push the Book through the portal."

"How do you annoy a book with every type of sex in its memory bank? A book that can make portals to other universes? Sounds complicated. Like being in the middle of an orgy with six men and trying to remember where you put your gum."

Zagan's eyes lit up.

The man was impossible. "Not that I've ever done that! But I can *imagine*. Complicated means more chances for things to go wrong."

Karl tsked. "We're going to make a herd of sex-crazed dino-shifters stampede and chew on the Necrosexi-texmexicon. Watch. Follow."

They dragged her out into the corridor and along to the fantasy romance genre where the book doors had titles like *Prophecy of the Twins*, *The Long Lost Prince*, and *We done followed the Trail of Clues and You're Saving Our Kingdom, Man.*

That last title ran all down the page and she ended up reading the final letters off the floor. It gave her a crick in her neck.

"These look good," Zagan shouted, from further along. He muttered as he walked, trailing his finger under the letters. "*The Lost Ninja Seal Team. The Found Mercenary King. The Orphaned Biochemist.* That's it!" He tugged open the door and they followed him into a city of dark alleyways, to a room where an oily-haired drunkard lolled on a bed. The man squinted at them while clutching his beer bottle.

"Who're you?"

Karl announced, "Your unwanted child from this unforeseen pregnancy will grow up to be the One Foretold who Saved the World from an Evil and Crazy Book."

He frowned and hiccupped once. "No shit? I thought this was the story where our biochemist daughter saves the world from a future plague?

His partner popped up her head from under the sheets. "Or the invading demon army?"

"Neither." Zagan shoved a document in front of the man. "Sign here, both of you, to release all rights to the baby."

"Why?" The man squinted.

Without more than a second's pause, Zagan transformed into a demon with flames pouring off him and Karl plopped out a random large tentacle that landed on the man's lap.

"*That is why.*" Zagan's voice rocked the room.

Virginia screwed a finger into her ear. *Ouch.*

"Good enough!" The man snatched the offered pen, hiccupped, and signed, as did the woman.

The following events happened in a rush – they departed the story and twiddled with the door knob. "Twenty years in the future...thirty years. This should be it!" Zagan declared.

They re-entered the book world and found a woman at an apartment. They quizzed her and, after confirming she was the same person as the baby and therefore also the...cue drumroll...*Orphaned Biochemist*, they rushed her to a laboratory.

Despite Virginia's screams of embarrassment, Zagan gave the woman Virginia's long lost panties and demanded she synthesize some chemical compound.

Time whizzed past in a montage of Bunsen burners and test tubes and people with goggles staring at things that bubbled.

Carrying a clinking bag filled with bottles and bottles of whatever the woman had made, they returned to the jungle-war book and exited through the tear in the world, to wherever it was that Mr. T. had gone.

Virginia clutched at her heart, which was pounding along so fast, she was sure it was a wasted moment of cardiac excitement. She should've been having desperate sex, or kissing at the very least. Racing hearts and sex went together like the flu and sneezing, like bikers and body shots, like blow jobs and mouth wash – or so she'd heard.

Dangerous Bob was here already, on the other side of the tear, standing at the top of a small rise. He was watching something through binoculars.

Where was this?

A distant scream then a roar chilled her blood.

She leaned her head toward Karl and whispered. "Where are we?"

"Cretaceous period in history. *Dinosaur Abduction by I. M. Horny.*"

"Uh-huh."

Here was green. More jungle-y than the last jungle, but it had an ancient air. The plants seemed different and bigger, which she figured was probably because this was millions of years ago before anyone invented weed killer. Something large buzzed in and tried to sink a proboscis the size of a hypodermic needle into her arm.

She swatted the bug, unscrewed it from her flesh while going *ow, ow, ow,* then flung the creature away. Dinosaurs roamed the earth along with fucking huge mosquitoes.

From the bushes, something crept. It pounced on the corpse of the mosquito and swallowed it. After blinking at her, the dead-bug swallower scuttled off.

She grabbed hold of Karl's arm. "Can we go elsewhere, please?"

We need to be there. As he swore, Bob pointed toward a distant herd of something big.

Everything was fucking big here.

He hitched the coil of electrical extension cords into a better spot on his shoulder, did the same with the belt for the twin Colt revolvers he'd found somewhere, in one of the stories, then he set off. All the men had found shirts too.

A pity that. Funny how she'd forgotten to find panties or something to wear on her bottom half.

"Crap. I'm sure that's further away than *elsewhere* should ever be." She considered telling them to leave her here, but at the snap of jaw and snarl of some hidden beast, she hurried to catch up. At least she'd found some gym shoes in the last book. And a frying pan. Which were totally more important than underwear.

Everyone had their chosen weapon and now she did too – strapped across her back like any legendary weapon should be. She stretched up her arm to check it was reachable...and couldn't touch it, no matter how she curved her arm. Or, or...this way maybe? This time she did a little *hop*, as if that would help. *Fuckit.*

"You okay there?" Karl looked perplexed.

"I'm fine." She snatched her hand down, smiled stiffly, and walked on.

He chuckled. "Virginia, you dork. Next time, when you find one lying about, *tak*e the damn singing ninja sword with the glowing blade and the Word of Power on the steel."

Her mouth turned down. "Smart ass. I was being honest, is all, and not stealing."

He swatted her butt. "You stole the frypan anyway."

Took another half hour before the sting faded. *Owie.* That man could swat. Besides, the frypan was good steel too and even had a word on it that was close to her name – *Virgin Steel.*

When they reached their destination, she had her frying-pan draw down pat and could get it out and ready for action within two minutes of gymnastic reaching.

"It's near here," Zagan whispered.

"What?" She stopped practicing, wiped sweat off her forehead, and looked up. From the nearby grunting and the pounding of the earth, she should've been watching where they were going.

"The Book. It's here."

Where? The copse of trees to the left, or the swamp to the right...or somewhere among the bunch of dino...saurs...having sex...with, what the fuck, with women? Gee whizzes. The things one learned.

She tilted her head one way and then the other, hoping to figure out how they did it without exploding the women. From the women's screams of joy, it was fun. But surely dino dick was huge?

Squinting didn't help. "Dangerous Bob." She put out her hand, palm up. "Binoculars, please."

He grunted, gave her a ton of advice along with a slew of swearing, but handed them over.

They didn't help either. Still impossible. *Concentrate. Concentrate.*

Big dick poised to go in – like, it was close to half as wide as the woman. Naked woman held by little dino arms, butt out. Dick in, disappears inside her. Out again and still visibly big.

Fuck. "Argh! I don't get it! Is this like some space time continuum warp where things are bigger or smaller than they appear? It has to be. If I keep looking, I will figure this out. Surely sometimes it goes wrong?"

Bob snatched away the binoculars.

"Hey! You're interfering with important schlong research."

"Leave it be, Virginia." Karl grasped one of her wrists. "The Necrosexi-texmexicon is watching too. We have to act now before it vanishes again."

"Besides," Zagan added, as he grabbed her other wrist. "If she goes pop you won't want to see. My fans do it sometimes, on the high riffs, and it's messy."

"Okay! I get it. Let me go then."

But instead they proceeded to hold her still as they stripped off her T-shirt, bra, and poppy stem skirt. She screeched a few curses at them but they didn't stop until she was naked. Then they let her go. If there was anything guaranteed to make her nervous, or maybe that should be *nervouser*, considering Bob was watching her and there were giant dino-shifters nearby...it was that Zagan and Karl were pulling off their shirts too.

"Hey, guys." She waved her hands. "No sex. Remember?"

"We're not." Only Zagan could say that with a straight face yet still look like he wanted to fuck her until she couldn't walk.

"That would be more reassuring if you weren't moving in on me. If we're not having public, dino-voyeur sex, why are we naked? Or mostly naked, in your cases?"

Hmm. Two men with bare chests. Sexy men. She had a sudden urge to sing out *I can see man titty* while doing a dance. Somehow, she was certain that would not end well.

"We're attracting the attention of the Book. Is it coming closer?" He jerked his head slightly backward. Swampward even.

Virginia went up on her tiptoes while still attempting to cover her pussy and breasts with her arm and hand. The swamp? What was there?

Something bright green that glittered caught her eye. "Oh damn. You're right!"

Could a book sneak? Because this one was. There was a moving *V* in the water behind where the peak of a green book cleared the surface. As she watched, it emerged until a few feet above the swamp. Weed and water dripped from it.

"When it gets to within throwing distance, say." Without taking his eyes off her, Karl rummaged in the long bag they'd brought with them that held several bottles of the biochemist's synthesized compound. "We're throwing these at it, so it has to be close enough to be accurate." He smiled, arching one brow. The aim of that look hit her at breast level. From the bulge in his pants, her standing within his reach and nude was going straight to his cock.

"I can do that, but..." She waggled her finger. "Don't be getting ideas." She lowered her voice to whisper. "Doing it once in front of Dangerous Bob was enough, thank you."

Bob chuckled and she shot him a glare. The man had the hearing of a bat.

"I thought it was supposed to have all combos of sex inside its pages. What's so special about us compared to the dinos essentially reboring the..." Pussy seemed wrong in this case. Hoohah trivialized what must be an amazing event that should really be in a science journal. She settled on science. "Reboring the vaginas of their cavewomen?"

Dangerous Bob squeaked and went instantly white, swaying as if he might topple at any moment.

Karl grabbed her again and slapped a hand over her mouth.

"You can't say that!" Zagan glared at her. "That's *verboten*, forbidden, out of bounds."

"Huh? Wha?" Freaky. He'd used German to get his point across. That meant this must be ultra-serious. Like using *ultra* in front of words, which was a cool, hip way of saying *super* when *very* would have been fine. Adjectives gave her the shits.

She focused down and contemplated Karl's hand across her mouth.

The rest of him was behind her. The rise and fall of his chest against her body stirred naughty thoughts. Where Zagan smelled of brimstone and sex, Karl was the depths of the ocean mixed with a hint of James Bond and a dash of marinara sauce.

What if she nipped him to get him to take his hand away? What would happen?

The idea tantalized her, like a dangling hook before a squirmy mermaid in heat.

Behind her, more than mere manly chest bumped her naked butt. Something hard was there. Something long. Her heart and breathing froze, as if to say, don't bother doing anything for a second, we need to assess the man and decide if we should do *it* with him.

Schlong alert grade ten and rising.

With his hands on his knees, Zagan lowered himself to her level, the heavy curve of his black horns advertising his masculinity. She swallowed, trying not to signal her awakening arousal. He said quietly but firmly. "You can't say vagina in a romance novel."

Karl nodded, his cheek scrubbing on her hair. He removed his hand.

Poking her tongue at her lip, Virginia turned over the logic, and saw the flaw in the argument. "What about penis?"

There was a thud off to the side, where Bob stood. Man, had he fainted?

CHAPTER 13

"Look what you did." Zagan crouched over the comatose Dangerous Bob. The flames running through his back and side markings flared hotter, a deeper orange. They always looked lickable to her. She hadn't had a chance to try the taste yet though.

"Me? You could throw a rock at him and it'd bounce. Why was me saying...that word so bad? Is he okay?"

"He will be. He's just allergic to the *p* word and the *v* word." After putting a peg on Bob's nose, Zagan unfolded to his full height. Which seemed to be some inches taller than before. Was he growing?

"You can't be allergic to words. Why the peg on Bob's nose?"

"You. That's why. And I guess you can be allergic. He is. He breaks out in a rash when he goes to the doctor's. Here. I think the scent is leaching out a bit. She's affecting you." He tossed a peg to Karl and clipped one on his own nose.

"Is that surprising?" Karl laughed, but he put the peg on, even as his other hand stayed resting reassuringly on her shoulder.

Had he noticed that she was breathing faster? "What do I have to do with pegs?"

A soft crunch and rustle, as if something waded through grass, came from the swamp area.

"Is it you-know-what?" Zagan did a not so subtle twitch of his eyes.

It was. The Necrosexi-texmexicon squatted in the short grass. Though its cover was shrouded in mud, from either side of the spine several red eyes, like cabochoned gems, watched them with all the eagerness of a creepy guy in a raincoat waiting for a peep show to start.

"It's...it's there. Close enough to throw a bottle, I think." Now what were they planning?

"Good. Here." After tossing five of the teeny tiny bottles to Karl, Zagan whipped around and lobbed about the same number at the book. More whizzed overhead, as Karl let fly.

They looked empty. Yet within seconds of them smashing against the hardback book, an odd scent reached her.

"What is that?" She wrinkled her nose.

"You. Your panties extract multiplied by ten thousand. Female pheromones guaranteed to attract any male within a mile!"

Gah. "Peg! I need one too! You're both going to Hell, you know!" This was so gross. She spun and went to grab Karl's peg but he intercepted her hand.

"Don't." Threat rumbled in his voice. "It should only affect us three or them." He jerked his head toward the dinos. "They should be here any minute. Besides." He smiled knowingly. "Zagan's been to Hell already and they spat him out."

The hazards of letting men figure out the strategies. "My panties," she muttered, rolling her eyes so fast she would swear she heard them squeak.

His *look* shut her down. As did his big fist in a *V* around her nape. She shuddered. That always sent a wave of *ohmigod* down her spine – better than a shot of raw Tequila.

Her man with the roaming tentacles clearly had ideas.

Maybe she should say no? Virgin card and all?

Her inner voice guffawed. *Lightning is going to strike us both if you keep that up, and I'm still getting the taser scorch-marks off my butt.*

She scrambled for some words to ward Karl off. Think badass bitch. "Really? My damn panties?"

"Shut up and let me kiss you, woman."

Well, if he put it *that* way...

Then he did it – planted on her a kiss deep enough and long enough to suck all the oxygen from the air and put out fires, if it hadn't instantly set her alight with lust. Small contradiction, but hey, in general, this fire was good.

When she came up to breathe, she found Zagan crowding her from behind then his hands descended, settling on her waist, as he nibbled a highway to love down her neck and her back.

"Don't move," Karl murmured. "Let him taste you, my pretty one."

Move? As if. Shivers of anticipation ran through her as each bite met skin. Her nipples bunched up small, tight and hard.

When Zagan parted her thighs and nipped the back of them, with his horns pushing into her butt, she almost came on the spot.

She heard a *psst* in her head.

Fuck. Her inner voice again? *Take a rain check. Back of the queue.*

The demon, with both hands anchored on her ass, was carpeting her bottom with teeth marks. Karl had resumed kissing her. There were tentacles arising. And cocks. Definitely those. A tentacle slithered around at belly height.

I can't take a rain check! I'm in your head. This isn't right. They're behaving oddly. None of you are watching the dinosaurs!

Having her inner voice shouting at her sent a spike of adrenalin through the system. Yet her head swam with lust, barely keeping above the oncoming sea of maleness, of raw sexuality. Both Karl and Zagan had stripped off the last of their clothes and they were doing *nice* things to her. Every bit of her that any girl would die to have nibbled on, or caressed, had been, and was.

No. Think. Must look. She ducked away from the next kiss and Karl transferred his kissing to her neck, his arms sliding around her back to keep her still.

Though gasping from what they were doing, she caught a glimpse of the dino sex arena. They were still at it. None were headed this way.

Common sense intruded. She wasn't a slut and doing this in front of... Okay, Dangerous Bob was currently undangerous but there was still an evil book watching.

"Wait, wait, guys." She wriggled loose and skipped backward under the trees where maybe she'd have a chance of dodging them. "Look. This is not normal. You're under the influence of my..."

They were moving in again, eyes filled to the brim with pure animal need.

Where were a chair and a whip when she needed them?

"Of your delicious female cream?" Zagan suggested hoarsely.

"Of your luscious sexy pussy honey?" Karl beckoned with his hands. "Come here, female. We want to fuck you."

"Ewwww!" She shook her head. "I'm not a dessert!"

Though she had an ugly spluttering moment over the sexy pussy honey line, she gathered her wits and decided to explain, carefully, walking backward while she talked. No need to tempt them.

"You need to think. Okay? Think. The pegs have fallen off your noses. You're under the influence of, ummm, me. Also, smell and taste are dependent on each other. You really should've worn face masks. The pegs were not enough. So, now that's settled," Her back hit a tree trunk and she stepped aside, "Now we can go and sit down somewhere comfy, have a cup of coffee...talk rationally, calmly. Guys?"

A tentacle whipped around her ankle, she tripped and sat down with a thump, and they swarmed over her. *Doofuses.* She managed a last grumbled question as they manhandled her. "So it's to be the two of you together then? Blancmange?"

Being in sex shifter mode always did make Karl lose a few brain cells. He stared at her, paused in the middle of tentacle wrapping her waist. "Huh?"

Zagan's forehead creased in thought for a count of one, two, three. "You mean ménage?"

She shrugged as well as she could. "Thought I'd stay with the dessert theme."

After one snort from Karl, she found herself held off the ground with her arms tangled up behind her while they licked her body, her breasts, her belly, then, at the last, parted her legs and something licked her clit, over, and over, and *oooh yum*, over again. *Melt.* What it was, she wasn't checking. If it wasn't a tongue, she did not want to know.

She squirmed and whimpered. This was utterly unfair, being outnumbered. Then she gave in and wiggled herself closer to that tongue thing. *Oh yes. There. And there too.* A climax thundered in nicely and she was still panting when they upended her.

Crap.

By the time they were done with her, she was upside down, blindfolded, her ankles were fastened a few feet apart to an above branch, and she had enough male attention to make a dyslexic postman want to deliver a letter to her slot.

Tentacles slid and slithered over her, wrapping and unwrapping themselves, probing and prodding, along with at least one cock doing the same to her mouth. Why were men so bad at aiming? She squeaked, panted, wriggled, but no matter what she did, they didn't stop. She had a cock in her mouth, something else worming into her pussy, what felt like a well-lubricated cock trying to breach the outer ring of her ass, and she had a strange feeling they weren't taking no for an answer.

Not that she wanted them to.

She made a gurgly, muffled noise as the one in her mouth began to travel back and forth across her tongue, filling her mouth deliciously.

She had a question on her lips that wasn't getting answered when she had her mouth occupied. The taste was reminiscent of demon not calamari. This had to be Zagan.

Her question: How many goddamned cocks do you guys have? Whatever the answer, she had an overabundance of them.

Then everything probing her managed to find its way in all the way at the same time, stretching her overwhelmingly, like a box of cookies with a few too many crammed in. Her mind fuzzed. She gagged, but in a good, stunned *whoah amazing* way. Her mouth fell open another quarter of an inch and she strained her thighs as if to let them enter her even deeper, if they so wished. Being upside down was doing things to her head. Somehow her question tiptoed quietly a long way away.

For a frozen moment she could only hear herself panting wetly around the cock, and the men panting also. No one moved, except for her impatient pussy as its muscles clamped onto the tentacle invading it, or the cock, whatever. *Fuck*, this felt good.

"Now I'm going to make you come so many times, I'll lose count," Karl grated out.

Not hard to do when he was shifted, and had a brain the size of a sea cucumber, but okay.

"And we're going to fuck you so hard you won't be walking for days." That was Zagan.

"Uh, guys," she gurgled and it came out *ughmmm*. She needed to walk. Seriously, it was a good if under-rated ability.

They almost did it too. From the second some mouth thing suctioned onto her clit and some fingers and tentacles wrapped around her breasts, she was arching into a mini climax. From the moment she was thoroughly taken over by her two males, she was done for. Orgasm after screaming orgasm was ripped from her, demanded from her, suctioned out of her like a golf ball down a really long hose. They took their own pleasure also, fucking her in so many ways and directions she was sure she'd need a Rubik's cube expert to reassemble her after.

The tree got cum on it, as did they, and her, surprisingly, along with some black ink that came off when they scrubbed her with leaves. When she roused herself after they let her down from the tree, rolling onto her side and propping herself up on her elbow, she looked over the top of Karl to find Dangerous Bob watching them with wide eyes. He had cum on him too from a branch above dripping onto his head.

She eyed the leaf as drips formed.

Drip. Drip.

Her inner anal freak wanted to tell him but she only twisted her mouth and decided to stay silent. If she said sperm he might faint.

Then she noticed other details. Her skin bore the marks of tentacle suckers as well as teeth. In a vast circle around them, the grass had been blown flat and further out was a circle of freshly fallen leaves.

In short, it had been awesome spermgasmic, tentacular sex.

Eek. The Necrosexi-texmexicon had sneaked closer too. Its red eyes were dulled and half-shut, its cover looked scuffed, and it sat in a shallow pool of white liquid that, on reflection, she did not want to ever see again. Even some depressions in the earth around it brimmed with the stuff.

The Book looked spaced out and overcome, in an orgasmic haze, perhaps. Safe, for the meantime.

Maybe, just maybe, they'd done something new to it after all? What were the chances that one of its pages detailed a ménage between a demon, a human and...whatever Karl was, a tentacle monster from another dimension?

She flopped onto her back and cuddled an arm from each of her semiconscious mates who lay to either side. *Wowie.* She was possibly not a virgin anymore.

A distant banging or drumming noise made her listen closely. "What's that?"

Groupies. Bob shrugged. *They found us and they're after Zagan. While you were doing it, I went and checked. They're outside the door but haven't figured out how to turn the knob.*

"What?"

He raised both shoulders in an, I have no idea why either, sort of gesture.

An idea sneaked in and clubbed her on the head. Only problem, her men had done what they'd said. Her legs were made of rubber.

"Dangerous Bob."

He grunted a *yes*.

"I have a mission for you. Listen carefully. The survival of the universe depends on you."

CHAPTER 14

While she waited for Bob to come back, the strength returned to her poor wobbly legs. She hunted down her clothes, T-shirt, bra, and poppy stem skirt, then she pulled and clipped them on.

The Book was snoring, as were her men. Waking Zagan or Karl seemed fraught with the possibility of them going sex-mad again and she needed to be free of pestiferous males to put her plan into action. Okay, cross that out, free of gorgeous men. Besides, they'd OD'd on her pheromones and would likely be worse off than her...considering how much cum they'd left on the undergrowth, the trees, on Dangerous Bob... She sighed. Everywhere really.

They probably needed IV infusions.

Meh, they were alien monsters and demons, they'd survive.

The crunch of footsteps alerted her. Bob appeared on the horizon, trotting toward her.

I propped the door open! They're not far behind. He gasped out a whole string of profanities as he reached her. *Here. This was all she could make. Something about demon sweat being hard to create.*

Shit. She hadn't thought of that. If her panties were good enough, she'd figured Zagan's shirt would be too. The tiny bottle held only a few opalescent drops. They seemed to sizzle when she held the bottle to her ear.

"Can you hit the book from here?" She held the bottle out to Bob. Maybe she could do it but she wasn't great at throwing. "Or we could sneak closer?"

He tsked, as if thinking then shook his head, mumbling out some fuckittys and fucks. *You haven't seen how vicious that thing can be. I'll get a little closer but you stay here. You should drape yourself on Zagan. I figure that's your best chance at disguising his scent. Hear that?*

A gentle thunder sounded, increasing in volume as she listened. The ground vibrated. "Sounds like a full-on stampede."

He cursed out the affirmative and spat to the side. *Yup.*

"Be quick." But she watched. She had to see. This was so important.

The vial hurtled towards the book, struck, and bounced to roll an inch or so from the cover. It hadn't shattered. Her heart lurched to a halt and she held her breath as Bob pulled out a pistol and shot at the vial. And shot some more. And missed some more. The man had as good an aim as a drunk on a pogo stick trying to hit a urinal.

The thunder of stampeding groupies grew louder.

"Damn." She looked at Zagan, then at the girls running toward them, arms waving. Screams of *Zagan* split the air and made a few frightened possums fall from the trees. Zagan. Book. Zagan. Which?

Fuckit. The world needed saving and he was a super-tough demon.

She sprinted toward Bob who'd almost emptied the second revolver. She tapped his shoulder. "Give it! I can do this."

Without a word, he gave her the pistol.

The Necrosexi-texmexicon was stirring, its eyes opening. It rose a few inches from the mud.

She unslung the frypan. Gun in one hand, frypan in the other. She held her breath again, and aimed, knowing this was the only way. It always worked in movies. She prayed that inside a story would be the same. The frypan seemed to emit a subsonic hum and turn a mildly exciting shade of luminescent purple. The words *Virgin Steel* glowed red-hot.

Must be time for her next eye check.

She squeezed the trigger.

The bullet caromed off the frypan and whizzed off toward the book, hit the one rock that was in the way, ricocheted, *peeeowww*, and smashed into the vial.

But when she looked over her shoulder, the girls had reached where Zagan and Karl lay. They milled about for a few seconds, sniffing, quietly screaming then the front runner sprinted toward

Virginia.

Dangerous Bob dragged her out of the way and the horde of groupies ran past.

"Zaaaaaggaaaaan!"

The Book disappeared under a writhing mass of girls. Legs, bottoms, and arms, waved and wiggled in the air. More and more groupies piled on.

Virginia put her hand to her chest. "Poor thing. I wouldn't want to be under that."

Bob laughed. The grin on his face said he'd consider it if offered.

Now, to wait and see. Would it make the portal? Would it even leave of its own accord?

Five minutes went past. The mass of girls and book had grown to ten feet high but had stabilized. The clock was ticking.

Tick, tock. Tick, tock. Tock. Tock. Tock.

Virginia reloaded and shot the clock.

Karl and Zagan awoke and came to stand beside her, yawning and stretching.

Twenty yards away, in the middle of the swamp, an electric blue portal fizzled into existence.

"We did it! Yay! Woohoo!" She jumped into the air then bounced about like a cheerleader with too many pom poms until Karl pulled her into his arms and snuggled her against him.

"Be still. You're making my headache worse. We need the Sea Wolves to come through anyway."

"Can you lure them somehow?"

"They know me. If they can they will follow my scent and return to this world."

She cocked a dubious eyebrow. *Eww* at the scent. Everyone here today was smelly. But, if it worked, it worked.

A moment later, they arrived – tumbling, stepping, and in Souleater's case, riding his Harley from the portal and into the swamp. An arc of mud sprayed from his tires as he wheeled about and rode their way. When the entire pack, herd, flock thing, she really *must* ask Karl for the right term, of bikers were gathered around her and Karl, she knew it was time for the final step.

She raised her hand, the one with the gun as it added to the drama. "Now we must return the Necrosexi-texmexicon to where it came from! Let's all push."

They strode forward in a determined line toward the ball of squealing and squirming girls.

"Your men are brave," she told Karl.

He smiled, examining their target. "Courage is never lacking in the Sea Wolves."

Dangerous Bob snickered and rubbed his hands together.

But where did you take hold? The huge mound of wriggling and now, *what the hell*, moaning, girls made getting a grip difficult. Why were they moaning?

"Maybe we need to try rolling? Does it matter if some of the groupies end up in another dimension?" She glanced at Zagan who was eyeing a few of the nearest and cutest butts on the girls.

Dayum. Men!

"Hey!" She snapped her fingers. "Concentrate."

"I am. I'm concentrating so hard my balls are going blue."

Everyone but her chuckled.

And that was when Prudence Prim arrived, her black stiletto boots sinking in the soft ground, her leather skirt just long enough to show a pert ass. Her baby hippo trotted at her heels, squeaking when it stepped in a soft patch. "What in the name of the Zon is going on here?"

"Obvious, isn't it." Virginia frowned. "Returning an evil book to where it came from. Plus a few odd groupies."

"Hmm." She stalked about, looking at the scene from various angles. "Wait. I need clarification." Then she squatted, helped the little hippo stand up on its hindquarters, and listened to whatever it said.

What was the world coming to when it depended on hippo philosophy? The weight of the pistol reminded her that she still held it. Maybe she should shoot the hippo? Or some groupies? It would lighten the gun.

You goin' crazee? Her inner voice asked. *Do that and I'm gone.*

Finally, it was doing its job. "Wasn't going to," she said quietly. "Just wanted you here to tell me what to do."

Silence.

I'll call the men with strait jackets now, shall I?

She smiled. "Just wait."

Prudence rose to her feet. "The decision is thus. No further persecution of this book will take place on Zon territory. We have decided it is a book of some consequence and it will be filed under its own genre, *Nasty world-shaking sex books,* until we decide otherwise. Unless it manifests a dirty cover which has boobies or man titty or other suggestive elements like handcuffs or crops. Ahem." Prudence hurriedly hid her crop behind her back. "If such naughtiness occurs then it will go into a dark corner to be buried under whatever crap we can think of. That is all." She picked up her hippo. "And now, I'm going back to my man that I have chained to my bed. Be good little Zonicans. Or else."

She clicked her fingers and vanished. The Sea Wolves seemed unsure what to do and looked at Virginia.

They couldn't touch the Book? She blinked, stunned. "What if it destroys the universe? Zagan? Karl?"

"Well." Karl rubbed his chin. "She has a point. It hasn't yet. Maybe it won't. And it is a book. It does have a place here, in a way. And the girls seem to have tamed it." He pointed.

One of its eyes was showing and somehow she sensed happiness in the glossy, rich redness of that weird eyeball. Dammit, the book was purring.

"Well then? We're done?"

"In a way." He looked over at Zagan. "Come on. We need to tell her."

"What?" But they wouldn't say another word to her until the three of them were alone under the trees again. She'd checked above before joining them. A clean area of trees, luckily. "Well? What is it?"

Somehow they'd made her nervous. Being nervous with a pistol seemed bad planning so she carefully set it on the grass and then, fumbling to find the right spot, she holstered her frypan too.

"I'll begin." Karl took up a solid stance. What seemed to be sadness passed across his face before he firmed his expression into his usual unreadable one.

Shit. "Is this something bad? As in badder than the world disappearing up its own ass?"

She indicated the Book, which was currently surrounded by a mob of dancing girls. It was even doing a bit of a jiggle as if wanting to join in. So odd. Virginia shuddered. Eye bleach needed soon.

"Luckily, we seem to have avoided that." Zagan shuffled his feet. "But there's us too."

"Us?" Why were they both acting suspiciously? "I thought we, as in all three of us, were now an *us*?"

"No." The flat statement from Karl rocked her.

"No? What do you mean?"

He continued. "No, as in we're too dangerous for you. Ever since we entered your life, my sweetness, you've been almost killed most days of the week. Zagan and I have decided we must set you free. We cannot be your mates anymore. I'm sorry."

"Yes." Zagan nodded, his mouth downturned. "I too am sorry."

For all of ten seconds, she looked from one of them to the other. This had blown her mind. Nothing was happening inside her head except an awful, eerie whistling. Empty. In her imagination, a cliff loomed closer, creeping in, like it was inviting her to throw herself off.

Fuck that. She'd beaten the Necrosexi-whatsicon all by herself. These two...fuck.

"Well, crap. Me too. I'm sorry too, boys."

They blinked at her. She'd never called them boys before, of course. But right now, they were acting just so...*stoopid*. Her anger boiled over.

Do eeet, said her inner voice.

For the first time ever, she smoothly drew her frypan. She whacked them both upside the head. The clang echoed. "If you two are ever this dumbass again, I swear I'll...I'll..." Fuming, she ground to a halt. She had nothing more and they knew it.

Zagan rubbed his head. "I think she means it."

"Yeah." Karl grinned. "I think it's love."

"You bet it is. You're not leaving me. Or else." She tossed the frypan to the ground. Tears rolled down her cheeks and she had to sniff.

"Damnation." Karl wrenched her into his arms. She heard Zagan step closer and he too joined the huddle.

"Shh. We have you. I won't leave."

The pats and the warmth of them surrounding her let her relax and she closed her eyes and sighed. "Good."

"You dented the frypan," Karl murmured next to her ear before kissing her neck.

"Also good. You can buy me a new one. It's the first sign of True Love."

She snuggled some more, resting her head on Karl's chest and squeezing her arm back to hold as much of Zagan as she could.

Her Quest must finally be complete. At last she had two ten-inch schlongs all to herself.

THE WELL-HUNG GUN

A kinky western spoof featuring John Beastwood, a hero with six guns and six tentacles.

While in search of a man-flu cure, Virginia trips on a nuclear powered skateboard and goes back in time to 1860. She marches into Peckerwood Springs determined to find her way back to her future.

If any damn were-squid gunslinger gets in her way, Virginia's gonna shove his nearest tentacle up his own whatsit.

Back to the future on acid, with a hefty dose of sex and tentacles.

CHAPTER 1

Virginia pushed past the junk piled to either side of the narrow room. On rickety shelves rested large dusty bottles, tubs so ancient the plastic had turned brown and the labels were moth eaten, and tubes of something called most efficacious unguent? Where and how was she supposed to find a cure for whatever illness Karl suffered from?

The dim light from the couple of light bulbs hanging from the ceiling showed the medicine room to be as modern as Frankenstein's laboratory.

Supposedly, she would just *know* what to grab. Sometimes Karl's superior dominant attitude made for annoying conversations. That he'd thrown the most recent cleaner off the castle roof meant no one was around to help. If she hadn't given them a parachute, they'd be splattered across the front driveway. All the bikers, from Dangerous Bob to Souleater to Horse, were off on a run collecting some shipment.

A faint glow at the back of the room drew her onward. She lifted the skirt of her blue dress, tiptoeing past a shelf bearing a skull and a preserved...she peered closer.

What the hell was that? Something long and white bobbed in a jar she'd knocked with her elbow.

Wrinkling her mouth, she jerked back. *Ugh.* A preserved cock?

Serve Karl right if she took that to him and pronounced it his cure.

All he seemed to do was moan, clutch the sheets to his chin, whisper about terrible, *terrible* pain, and sniffle. If it was a man cold –

Her ankle banged into something rocklike. "Ow! Fuckit."

Hopping and holding her ankle, she barged into the shelf on her right, knocking loose papers and sending tubes sliding. One tube ended up under her hopping foot, then her next hop landed on something else that slipped. She hurriedly went to plant her sore leg on the floor. The thing underfoot hummed. A bright orange light flared.

Eyes wide in panic, she glanced down. *A skateboard?*

It rocketed forward, scattering everything, sending papers, jars, and dust flying in a tornado of weird medicines. The bottled cock floated past her face. The entire room flared an eye-burning blue then vanished with an obliterating...silence.

The skateboard was still vibrating under her feet, as if it were glued to her sandals. Air washed past, fluttering her long hair behind her. She could see nothing but black.

"Damn, Karl," Virginia muttered. "What have you gotten me into this time?"

If this involved more radioactive blow jobs, she might just kill Karl when she got back...if he hadn't already died from whatever it was afflicting His Supreme Tentacled Monsterness.

*****

Yellow light blasted across her vision. In one startled inhalation, she took in the smell of sun-baked dirt, cow dung, and air so dry it couldn't have rained for months.

The skateboard wobbled and bumped creakily across the uneven ground then stopped.

There were cactuses galore too. Where was this?

Many relevant questions ran through her head. Like...was it cactuses or cactii? How did she know what cow dung smelled like? Why were deserts so dirty and cactus-y?

No water. No food. Trapped, far, far away from home. To survive here, in this hostile moonlike environment, she'd need to be on the ball.

Wait. Maybe this *was* the moon?

She looked about some more. No astronauts. *A pity.* Scratch that idea. But she needed to figure out where she was and every possibility erased took her closer to the answer.

It wasn't Walmart either.

Whatever this contraption was, and it looked like an ordinary skateboard, it had travelled somehow, somewhere. It had brought her here, miles from where she'd been. Even the time of day seemed wrong. Scary thing, but she might need it to get back.

She stepped off the skateboard, picked it up, and tucked it under her arm. A startled bleep emanated from it, and red writing in miniature ran across the middle, before it went quiet.

She turned on the spot.

"Fuuuck," she whispered, as if the empty land was listening. The sky was still, cloudless, and the palest of washed-out blues.

Beyond, in the sky above a small hillock of dirt specked with yellow grass, vultures flew slow, menacing circles. Watching all those westerns with Karl had finally paid off – vultures meant dead things. Dead things might be icky, but they might also mean water bottles, food, maybe a cellphone?

This place seemed a long way from nowhere. No car engines revved in the distance. No power poles, no roads. Nothing but her and the suspected dead thing.

A vulture dived earthward and she broke into a jog.

On the other side of the low mound was a man staked out and spread-eagled on his back. Though his clothes were still on and someone had constructed a lean-to shelter over him, he looked like he wasn't getting loose anytime soon.

She sucked on her lip – an old habit that popped up when she was unsettled.

John Wayne and a hundred westerns meant she *knew* what was right. Wasn't he supposed to be smeared in honey and stretched naked over an anthill? This was like seeing one flower out of place in a perfect arrangement. For all of five seconds, she stood, arms at her sides, clenching and unclenching her fists. She itched to shift him a few yards over to *there*, where a busy ant hill prospered.

Going nuts, Virginia. *Help the man.*

Besides, there was a distinct lack of honey.

Fuck. It was PMS time. The man was lucky she didn't claw him to shreds with her nails, due to her having chipped one, seriously badly, during the trip here.

The reminder had her holding her splayed fingers before her eyes. A whole chunk was missing.

Nails? What the hell?

She detested manicures. Didn't really care about nails.

But Karl had sent her here, somehow, even if he wasn't anywhere near her when it happened. Karl. Mr. Man Flu of the year. And it was fucking hot. The sun was frying her neck. Sweat dribbled.

Nothing was where it should be! Including her.

Bees arrived in a ginormous imaginary hive, and took up residence inside her head, buzzing. Everything went just a little hazy and a lot red and black.

She needed to kill someone.

Breeeeeathe. Where was a paper bag when she needed one?

A few calming breaths later, she approached cautiously.

"You okay there...uhhh." What did you politely call a staked out man? "Mister?"

"Woohoo. Pretty lady. Whatever would you be doing out here? Name's Rafe. What's yours?"

Why not. "Virginia Chaste."

Cute looking. Red hair. A bit dusty and slightly pink of face but well built, like a man who worked hard for a living. She inspected the rest of him. Cowboy boots, *leather ones*, cowboy pants with a large crotch bulge that made her want to do an immediate schlong stat assessment...no, nah-uh, move on...cowboy shirt and what looked like a for real Colt revolver in a leather holster, on a frickin cowboy leather gunbelt.

Lots and lots of leather. She had a thing for leather. She sniffed. *Mm-mmm.* Much more than this and she'd OD.

It all said cowboy with a capital C – one scorched into a rawhide map with a branding iron.

She frowned, met his eyes. "Is this a movie set? Are we being filmed or something?"

"Filmed? What? What's that? Have you been too long out in the sun?" He clicked his tongue. "Untie me and I'll fetch you to the town doctor, lil lady." He jerked at the wrist ties. "C'mon. The men just left me out here while they get their first pokes in at the whorehouse."

"A whorehouse?" Wasn't that old west slang?

"Yeah. Whorehouse. Place where men get to poke loose women."

Poke. All she could think of was facebook. Poking there was decidedly unsatisfactory and nothing to do with whorehouses unless you happened to poke a Kardashishaggin sister.

Had to be a movie. Any minute someone would yell *cut.*

A vulture that'd been observing from off to the side made a quick swoop onto Rafe's chest. It perched there and aimed a peck at his eyes. Without faltering, Rafe darted his head forward and latched onto the vulture's neck with his teeth. A few meaty gnaws later, with the vulture squawking and flapping its wings, and the bird lay dead on his chest. Feathers floated groundward.

Oh myyy... What the...

Virginia rushed over and untied the leather bonds, freeing his arms. He sat up and reached for his legs.

"Thank you kindly. They were comin' back for me before sundown but this way I get to some whores before they is all plumb worn out."

"The vulture?" She fluttered her hand at the limp carcass that had rolled from his chest to the ground.

"It's dead. Damn thing shoulda known better than to come near my teeth."

Animatronic? The blood and feathers said no. Was it animal cruelty if you chewed through the neck in two seconds flat?

Not going there. *Ew, ew, ew.*

Rafe dusted off feathers and slowly stood, unfolding to a full...five foot three. She squinted downward. Maybe this film was being authentic? Weren't men shorter back then? Accidentally, her gaze drifted. Crotch bulge. *Jeez.*

Nine point five inches...and growing.

"You wouldn't by any chance be one of Madame Betty's new whores? Come in on a stagecoach and lose your way somehow?" The hope in his voice was bright. "Like a ride before I takes you in? Standing up, lying down, 'gainst a wall even, if there was one in the near locality."

Dumbfounded, she stood with her mouth fallen open.

He picked up his hat from the ground then pronounced his next words with it held in front, in both hands.

"I would enjoy parting your downbelow petals and sliding my shaft of joy inside your bounteous lady garden, Miss. May I?"

"Uhhh."

"See, I been out on a cattle drive fer months and the poor thang needs to let off before it exploderates in my pants." Rafe licked his lips and fidgeted, then he forged onward in a monotone like he was reciting poetry in front of a scowling audience. Granted, the scowling was true. "I guarantee an ocean of lust will be released by the union of our loins and sweep us into a land where you will find such joy as you have never known. Ahem." He rotated his hat a few times, standing there grinning with teeth showing.

Virginia hesitated. Such an enthusiastic boy-man. So eager. So in need of admission to a mental hospital.

Bounteous lady garden? Petals?

She was torn. Which impulse should she obey? Hit him with the skateboard and tie him up again? Or get out a hoe and do some weeding?

Perhaps encouraged by her stunnedness...Virginia frowned, that absolutely *was* a real word...he sidled up.

The skateboard bleeped and big letters ran across it.

Warning. MORON PROXIMITY ALERT.

"Really?" she muttered. "As if I didn't know."

Great. The skateboard talked.

Rafe looked bemused at her five seven height but he kept on sidling forward until what was definitely a superb erection nudged her dress.

The man had no shame. Though her brain had rung with silence at his words, Virginia was now struggling not to giggle.

In the old days, a nine point fiver would've had her drooling, but after Karl, no. Her search for the rare ten inch schlong had already borne glorious fruit.

"I'm taken...sir."

And you're so short I'd need to do you with you standing on a stack of dead vultures.

"Just lead me to this town where I can find a phone. Wait, can I borrow yours?"

"My what? Foahwen?" He said it like phone was a foreign word. Talk about staying in character.

"Mmhm."

"Don't have one. Is it some newfangled thing you whores are using?" Rafe grinned.

"I am not a whore!" Frustration boiled over into anger. "It's a phone! Not a fucking dildo strap-on something! Take me to your town before I shove your damn nonexistent cellphone up your ass!"

"Whoa." He stepped back, eyes wide. "Hold on there, Miss Pretty. I ain't aiming to do whatever you just said. Though I'm sure back in whatever place you come from it's all fine and dandy. My ass does not need nothing, there, at all."

She stood glaring.

"Noth-thing. Never, ever."

She grunted, glared some more, stamped her foot.

"Just one thing." His voice squeaked. "If you're not a whore, would you by any chance be a mail order bride for John Beastwood?"

"No!"

He gulped. "Okay. I'll take you to Peckerwood Springs. Just don't blame me if John takes a liking to you and drags you into his lair." He swiveled on his cowboy heels and set off.

Finally.

Sometimes PMS had its uses.

She muttered through her clamped jaw, "Whoever the heckitty this John Beastwood is he'd better watch his step or I'll imbed a skateboard in his skull."

Bleep.

This device is not to be used for physical assault.

Her growl made the red lettering vanish. The skateboard vibrated.

She frowned, staring at the thing, but it was silent and not talking. Scared of her? Good. All things should be scared of her on This Day of the Worst Ever PMS.

What the hell was with the *heckitty* anyway? This cowboy shit was infectious.

*****

A good old western town came into view as they topped a rise. The light was failing, the sun breasting the horizon, and the shadows were long. She peered down. Saloon. Bank. Sheriff. Lots of timber houses, dirt streets, horses. Creepy three story mansion reminiscent of Dracula's abode? Hmm.

The cameras were so well hidden she was going to grow eyes on stalks if she didn't spot them soon.

"Like her?" Rafe gestured. "Peckerwood Springs. Built thirty years ago in 1830 at the behest of John Beastwood's father. Started out as a ranch, then they mined awhile, then when the ore petered out, it became this modern cit-teee."

All hundred or so houses?

Something wrong with what he'd said. Maths, where was it when she needed it? 1830 plus 30 equaled 1860?

"It's nice. Are you bad at adding up by any chance?"

"Me? Why no. I am an *ex-cell-lent* numerologist, if I do say so myself. Thirty pokes and twenty pokes is one helluva sore dick. See?" He was still laughing as he took off at a trot toward the town. "Woohoo!" He did a leap and clicked his heels.

The man was too fucking happy.

Movie set. He was getting away from her and yet still he cackled. She gritted her teeth, lifted her dress to make it easier to run, and followed Rafe. She even managed to stop wishing for a Winchester rifle to stick up his possibly virgin ass.

On the way down the slope, she decapitated a cactus with the skateboard.

Because. Just because.

CHAPTER 2

She caught up to him and managed quite well at not beheading Rafe, despite his crazy grin when he found her running alongside. Dealing with the cactus had let her lose some of the homicidal annoyance.

"Never knew ladies could run like that," he hollered at her, one hand on his hat, the other holding up his gun belt.

Chauvinistic pig. She poked out her tongue and sprinted past him. With a whoop, Rafe sped up and they ran side by side.

As they reached the edge of town, hoof beats thundered closer and closer from behind. Rafe yanked her aside and they huddled against a building as seven men rode past. Many weapons hung from their belts – pistols, knives, and sabers. They rode straight in the saddle, with set mouths, and the froth from the mouths of their steeds flew like the rain of demons. In other words, some of it landed on her face.

"Fucking ew." She wiped the horse spit away. Horses were icky. She'd probably get herpes from this.

They drew and held aloft silver guns. There was evil intent in their demeanor; either that or she needed glasses. Alas, she couldn't behead all of them with a single skateboard.

Bleep.

Yay.

The word sped in red letters across the board.

She raised her eyebrow, staring at the skateboard. Was this thing reading her mind?

No.

"Phew. Thank heavens for that. Waaait. I'm not that naive, not anymore, not after doing blow jobs on a demon rock star whose cock resembled the space shuttle. Are you sure you're not reading my mind?"

She shook the board, thinking maybe it was like an etcher sketcher and would come clean if she jiggled its digital brain.

Yes, I am sur-u-ure. St-op-op do-ing that.

"Oh." She smiled. Her torture had worked. "Good."

The SPCS is going to hear about this.

"The what?"

She ran through the abbreviation in her head. Society for the Prevention of Cruelty to –

"Hey!" Rafe had barred his arm across below her breasts to hold her against the building so she wouldn't be trampled. Or so she had thought. His hand was doing some extra feeling. "Stop that."

"Oh. Sorry. I'm a little deprived." He gave her boob a last squeeze then stepped away to peer down the street. "Damn bandits. They're robbing the bank. It's clear all the way."

"To?"

"The whorehouse. Where else?"

They sneaked forward.

"Peckerwood Grand Parade." He swept his arm out, indicating the length of what seemed to be the widest street in the town.

Guns began firing. People screamed. Horses galloped up and down the main street, churning up dust. To her left, some of the invaders mounted their horses and turned them. *Bank* was written across the building beyond. A woman lay draped across one man's saddle.

As they whipped their horses into a gallop, heading straight for her and Rafe, townsmen appeared. From rooftops, doorways, and windows they aimed at the bandits. Guns blazed, sparks flowering from the muzzles, showing bright in the gathering darkness.

"Excuse me!" A grey-whiskered man led a horse with cart attached across the end of their street, blocking the exit. At the last second, Rafe dashed through the gap.

"Be seeing you Miss Pretty!" He ran off. "The whores are calling me!" Ducking and rolling, he headed across the bullet-laced street toward a two story building with fancy red curtains and fancy music spilling into the air. Even from where she stood, the smell of sex was heavy and the whorehouse seemed to pulse like a giant timber heart.

There was a sign out the front, all in pink.

THE FURRY TACO

Okay. Fine. She was in the middle of a gun battle. Hot lead was flying. Men were presumably dying, from the body that had just rolled off a roof to land with a great splash in a horse trough. And her advisor had escaped.

If this was modern day USA she'd eat a grilled gopher with mayo on a cactus sandwich.

Dayum.

Virginia stuck a knuckle in her mouth and bit down. "*Ow!* How am I supposed to get back to my own...time?"

Bleep.

Find a power source to repower me fully and I will return you.

"Oh. Cool."

Well, that was good to know.

But first you must complete your mission.

"Mission. What mission?"

To find a cure for Karl's disease.

"Seriously?"

Seriously.

She was going to kill Karl.

"Don't mind me." The old man crawled under the cart, pulled out a bottle, and gulped down several swigs. His burp sizzled the air, and the inside of her nose, sterilizing everything in its cloudy path. Cross-eyed, she watched a large dirt-smeared pig trot up, grunting. It squirmed under the cart and nosed the man.

"Ermitrude!" He patted her as she wriggled even closer.

The gun battle battled on.

Peeyow. Spang. Boom. Etcetera etcetera.

No one seemed to be dying at the moment, as the bandits had dismounted and hidden behind various things that when she thought real hard about them, could never ever stop a bullet more powerful than a sneeze.

Dammit, would someone please die? She yawned.

A strange jangling sound, like spurs being used as a musical instrument, made her look to the left. The building she was using for cover, the one they'd leaned against, was the Dracula mansion. On the porch was a rocking chair. A man sat in the chair, slumped, rocking slowly, with a Mexican blanket draped across him. His eyes were shut, and a black hat was pulled low at the front.

He was asleep, in the middle of all this?"

Rat-at-tat-at-ta-at-tat. Totally not a machine gun sound.

More bullets zinged about, also missing everyone, though a little old lady had an apparent heart attack and spun into the street clutching her chest.

As if making sure no one had missed the significance of her illness, she gasped out, "My heart!"

A paper bag dropped from her hand. When it hit the ground, popcorn flew.

"Oh my." She went to run out, only a young boy was already there, dragging the woman to safety.

"Don't worry about her. She just likes the attention." The old man added, in a hushed voice. "That there, on the porch, it's John."

"John Beastwood?"

"Uh huh. Best get under here with me."

She cocked a disbelieving eyebrow at him. "With you?"

"And the pig. Erma gets nasty when people push her about."

"You are?"

"Ornery Ol' Bastard."

Virginia chuckled. "I meant your name."

"That's it." After taking a swig from the bottle, he folded out a lapel of his vest to show a dull silver star pinned to his shirt. "Sheriff Ornery Ol' Bastard, at your service, Miss..."

"Virginia Chaste. I'll stay standing, thanks." She'd had enough of being felt up by the men here, especially ones who cuddled up to pigs.

The music jangled again, with added gusto and trumpets. A wind blew tumbleweeds down the street. The firing ceased. The air grew chill.

"Brrr." She really should've brought a sweater. Next time she time travelled, she'd pack.

Now...who was going to die?

With a jangly crescendo of trumpets, a huge horse leaped from the second story of the mansion. Flinging aside the blanket, John Beastwood stood. Immense, and tall of stature, he was a bare foot short of the ceiling. As he spun, his black coat flared open, revealing a glinting ammo belt and a whole damn arsenal of six-guns. While the horse trotted to a halt, snorting, she counted.

Six," she whispered. "Six six-guns?"

The man, his jet black hair curled and whipped by the wind, turned his head and *saw* her.

Her throat squeezed in, as if held by one of his black gloved hands. Definite wardrobe color thing going on there.

Her thoughts jolted to an abrupt halt. Her inner voice gasped and fainted.

Wait. The girl was back? Where had she *been*? Oh yeah, she'd forgotten – holidays. Who'd have thought she'd miss her?

Her breath came in shudders too.

Oy! The man? Her inner voice insisted.

Nice man. Big man.

Her heartbeat did a swift *pitter patter* then went in reverse.

Was that even possible?

Those four extra-strong cups of coffee this morning had come back to haunt her.

This man, this John Beastwood, had glowing *red* eyes, a jaw strong enough to make a woman swoon, and a chest broad enough to make her want to lean her cheek on him and caress it while smiling and going *yummm*. Also possibly broad enough to ricochet cannon balls off of. That broad.

Schlong stats, schlong stats, screeched her revived brain.

Too dark, for the shadows had gathered in his groin. Lucky things.

He turned away from her and the magic of his presence lessened a smidge.

She prayed he'd do the flaring coat thing again so she could see his ass.

To the left, the far distant left, the bandits rose from their cover, guns lifting and pointing her way, at the very big and obvious target of John Beastwood.

"Oh no!" She covered her mouth with her hand.

Bleep.

Duck.

At the same time as the skateboard's warning, the sheriff grabbed her leg and hauled her under the cart.

CHAPTER 3

Virginia had just enough time to wriggle out from under the cart and look up to see John Beastwood blur.

A threshing machine had nothing on him. A black wind seemed to cloak him, whirling, masking his movements, sending thick tendrils swishing. Gusts whisked her hair against her face, part blinding her. Dirt pattered the cart.

Six silver guns rose...well steel really but who was doing metallurgical analysis at this point in the story, right? All six of them fired, sending bullets raining down on the bandits.

No mere *pee-yows*, these went *blam, blam, blam*. Her ears rang. The pig cowered against her, nudging its snout under her armpit.

The sheriff had his fingers planted in his ears. Smart man. As the barrage continued, she did the same.

Just for the heck of it she counted. *Six, seven...twenty-two...hundred and one. My, my, these six guns held a lot of bullets.*

Bandits coughed, jerked, spun, and fell to the earth, expiring in most dramatic ways. Their boots twitched.

A few cried, "Ay carumba, you got me!"

The bank behind them slowly crumbled. First, the sign swung loose at one corner, then it toppled. The door sprouted a zillion holes, imitating Swiss cheese, and fell off.

Blood blossomed across the bandit's shirts, gushed upward, spewed earthward, and blew in thick gobbety rain on the air.

The sheriff passed her some popcorn.

Considering there were no streetlights and it was dusk, she was seeing this terribly well. The carrots were paying off. By the time he stopped firing the townsfolk had lit a few lanterns and were sitting out on porches.

The last bullet sang down the street then, as if by magic, one bandit appeared from a side street, galloped for the cart she hid under, and launched his horse overhead, landing with a great *ka-thumpitty* on the other side, and galloping some more, into the sunset. Virginia frowned, didn't the sunset used to be on the other side? She guessed this was more dramatic.

"That's it!" Though swaying, the sheriff helped her out from under the cart.

"Thank you, Sheriff..."

"Just call me, Sheriff Bastard." He yelled aside. "You missed one, John!"

"I know. I ran out of bullets." The man on the porch turned and stepped down onto the dirt. His casual stride brought him to within a yard of Virginia. His huge stallion trotted over and whickered.

"I need you to get him for me." John unsheathed a rifle from where it was strapped beside the saddle. It was long, with a golden buttplate, with some highly fandangled sight on top. "Catch."

Jehosophat. He even smelled better than coffee.

Would it be presumptuous of her to bite that bicep through his coat sleeve, now that he'd leaned it on the cart strut sticking up beside her?

Distinctly panting, her inner voice butted in. *Down girl, you're spoken for.*

Though he barely glanced at her, she felt as if John Beastwood was very aware of her presence, same as a mouse might know when a cat was playing and thinking of pouncing.

Pounce on me. Pounce.

Psst. Karl would not be happy.

Now she recalled why she'd let her inner voice go on holidays. The thing cramped her style. Yes, she was spoken for, but that was in the future. Karl did not exist in the here and now.

Cheating still.

She ignored her inner voice. Things were happening. The sheriff had been tossed the rifle and though he dropped it on his toe, he was now screwing another sight behind the one that was already attached.

"Gosh darnit, John. This is going to be a real doozie of a shot."

"You can do it." That baritone murmur coming from behind her, and barely a foot away, shook her all the way to her panties.

Her nipples peaked so hard they'd soon be digging their way through the cart timber she leaned on. If ever she'd gushed arousal, it was now. Her lady garden was getting a real good watering. Someone had possibly installed a new irrigation system.

Ew. Ew. Ewww.

"Shut up," she hissed at her inner voice, accidentally saying it out loud.

"Excuse me?" *He* leaned in closer and placed his other hand on the cart to her *other* side.

Which meant he'd boxed her in. *Fuuuck.*

"Did you speak, Miss?"

"I was, uh, clearing my throat?"

"Hmmm. Sheriff, need anything?"

"Nothing you can get me. He's over a half mile away now." A squeaking sound came as he adjusted some doozywhatsit on the sight. Then he took out his bottle of liquor and gulped down a few swallows. "I just needed some of this, and Erma."

His whistle brought the pig sauntering closer. Ermitrude flopped at his feet and the sheriff kneeled and propped the rifle on her side, aiming through the cart wheels toward the desert.

Whatever was he aiming at? A small black speck on the horizon was all she could see.

"Goood girl, Erma." He blew on his hands, adjusted some more screws, threw a feather in the air, said an incantation, and settled his hands on the rifle like he was holding his lover. At the same time as he squeezed the trigger, John placed his hands over her ears.

The *boom* still made her ears ring like a church bell.

Sheriff Bastard counted quietly, "Five, four, three, two..."

In the distance, the black speck halted. Was that a geyser of red coloring the skyline?

"Bingo. This old gun is like a dangblasted cannon."

"Told you, you could do it." John clapped his shoulder. As he moved, his body squashed hers to the cart, until a second later, when he shifted away.

Virginia swallowed, trying desperately to ignore the throbbing in her downstairs orchard.

Why are you thinking in weird metaphors? Her inner voice whispered.

It's your pussy!

How the fuck should she know? All these cowboys must be warping her mind.

Maybe it was the leather? John had on an ample amount – leather gun belt, leather boots, leather pants belt...she sniffed and detected an underlying fragrance beneath his yummalicious essence of male cowboy...possibly leather underpants?

Ever so slowly, she turned, finding herself still framed either side by his arms. Fainting would be bad.

Just keep breathing, just keep breathing.

Wide-eyed she waited for him to quit staring down at her. The red in his eyes had faded to mere pinpricks of fire, here and there, in his dark irises.

"Well hello, beautiful. Would you happen to be one of my mail order brides?"

One of? "Uhh. No?"

"Not sure?" He smiled dangerously in the way a shark smiles as it opens its mouth to eat a little fish. His dark curls seemed to do more curling than mere hair tussled by the wind should ever do.

Shark repellant needed ASAP.

CHAPTER 4

"Perhaps you'd like to come to supper with me, tonight?" John raised her hand and kissed the back, and his focus varied not one iota from staring at her.

Bleep.

Danger. Danger.

She'd propped the skateboard on the cart's wheel and could just read that warning without getting a cricked neck.

She had to say no. Didn't she?

"No?"

"No? You seem so unsure about everything I ask you."

"I mean, no. As in, no. Umm. No, no, and no. That clear enough?"

He kissed her knuckles again and smoothed his thumb over them. "I'll tell you tomorrow after you wake up in my bed."

A whisper of sensation made her look inward, dubiously registering...something, that may or may not have slithered under her dress to slide over her inner thigh, heading upwards.

Yikes.

She checked. Yes one of his hands was out of view...but the angle seemed impossible. Whatever was down there? Was there anything? Were there snakes in this desert? The feather-light touch sneaked under her panty elastic, brushed across her moist pussy lips, and snuggled inward a tad.

Her knees threatened to buckle.

Ohhh. Kerfuckitty.

If it was a snake and it bit her, leastways she could be sure Beastwood would suck the poison out.

"So." His voice dropped so many octaves, so fast, it'd give an orchestra hernias trying to hit the note. "Are you coming?"

Mmm. Coming? Her clit was close to vibrating in tune with his voice. Whatever mystery thing was in her panties needed to leave ASAP before she did something embarrassing.

Change the subject. The price of eggs in China? How to knit cock warmers? *Eep.*

A frantic scramble through her thoughts had her spitting out, "Love your guns. Silver?"

"Platinum-plated silver and steel with diamond encrusted accessories."

"Nice." *Go away thing in my panties.* Did it just wriggle?

"I could buy half the territories and states of the US of A with the proceeds from their sale."

Unfair! She panted, her eyes glazing over. Rich as well as handsome, sexy and menacing, *and* he boasted about his money? Someone had stacked the deck. She bit back a whimper.

For some reason her brain chose to ponder about his shooting prowess. How had he managed to fire six six-guns at once? Was he simply so fast, her eye hadn't registered the movement?

Yes, that. Of course. And totally irrelevant to the *now*, so why had her mind gone there?

Her inner voice muttered something like *can't fix stupid* and took up knitting cock warmers in a corner at the back of her mind.

She wrenched away her hand from his and tried to sidle out from under him, but he was leaning over her, like a mountain about to avalanche all over her body, about to wreak unnatural havoc on her breasts, about to kiss her like hot lava caressing a deforested slope. And boy, if he wanted to do some excavation and bore out her entrance, she'd hand him a mining contract.

Virginia clutched at the cart and croaked out, "Your question. Still no."

The thing below, that she still wasn't quite sure was there, slipped away, leaving her clit pulsing.

If she ground against him while he only watched, and had a teeny, tiny orgasm, would it be bad?

Yes!

Darn. Her inner voice needed tasering...again.

Tasers no longer exist, yet. Nyah. Nyah.

The mangled tense of that sentence made her squint with one eye and twitch.

John frowned and backed away. "Are you okay?"

Your chance! Take it. Run! "Ermm. My medications are overdue. I'm prone to conniptions and palpitations of the female kind." She smiled, toothily.

He tsked and did more frowning. "Sounds infectious."

"It is. Very."

"Perhaps another time then." He swept off his hat and bowed, then stalked away, to take the steps to his porch in one stride then enter his dwelling. The door shut. The whole town seemed emptier.

For the first time she noted the magnificent flower bed before his house. It stretched either side of the steps. Rosebuds nodded in the breeze, moonlight etching the petals in silvery pink and blood red.

"He's a bit of a gardener, our John. Best not to touch his flowers." The sheriff arched his back as he climbed to his feet and she heard a series of clicks. "Ahhh. That's better. Miss Virginia, I suggest you seek a place to stay the night. Peckerwood is a bit of a mess at the moment and the hotel manager has been shot and possibly drowned, so I doubt you'll get a bed anywhere except there." He indicated the whorehouse. "Madame Betty is a fine woman, if a little brusque. May I escort you?"

"Umm." She stooped and picked up the skateboard again. What was she supposed to be doing?

Finding a cure for Karl Thulhu and a power source for me!!!!

Blearily, she read the writing. What an insistent skateboard. Yes. But that would have to wait until morning. She was dead tired. "Lead on, sir."

The brothel, *whoops*, whorehouse, was clean inside and already busy with many leather-clad cowboys. A pity her weariness overrode her leather fetish. Her eyelids were closing as she listened to the sheriff arrange a room.

Madame Betty was big and wide, and that included her breasts. The size of those zeppelin balloons meant she was probably capable of smothering a man who got too close, yet her tatas were up front and bouncy.

How?

She tilted her head sideways, checking for some amazing undercarriage boob support. But no, under the bodice area of her dress, not a crane or cantilever was to be seen, not a single steel beam was in sight.

"Are you okay, Miss?" Madame Betty was following her head tilt with some concern. "The poor girl is going to keel over any moment. Carry her upstairs for me, Sheriff. She'll have to have the one next to a busy room, but it's got a feather bed and a view of the main street. Last room to the right."

"Okay dokey. Here we go."

She was snoring on the way up the stairs and barely noticed his arms under her, except that one time he staggered and almost tossed her over the rail.

The bed was indeed soft and feathery. Her eyes slammed closed like a bank vault. No one was getting in, not even Mr. Beastwood and his invisible hand.

"Zzzzzz."

CHAPTER 5

Her dreams haunted her, as did the squeak of bedsprings.

"Regale me with some of your purty words, Henry."

"Your wish is my command. Miss Candy. Lemme see... Your delicate flower reminds me of a taco once made for me by Pancho Villa himself. Pink, squishy, and, I do believe, very tasty. Jus' let me have a lick to check."

A squeal rang out. "I do declare, Henry. You have outdone yerself."

"Not yet I ain't."

Time blurred into blackness. The night was divided up by the ticks and tocks of a very loud clock, by bedspring squeaks...and by more noisy dreams.

"What's that, Henry?"

"A corn cob."

"An' what're ya planning to do with it?"

"Stick it up here."

Shrieks then giggles filtered in. "Henry! Extra for that, ya know. 'Sides, you'd need something to grease the way."

"Horse linament do?"

"No! That'd make my ass burn like hellfire."

"Axle grease?"

"Hell, no!"

"How 'bout lard...wait, I can get freshly churned butter from the kitchen. You just wait right there. Miss Candy."

Feet pounded down a stairway.

Virginia blinked. Or were they dreams?

Who knew whores would be so into cooking in the middle of the night?

Grumbling, she stuffed her head under the pillow and fell back into sleep.

Hours later, morning forced its way into her room, shooting spears of light through the red lace curtains and generally making a nuisance of itself. She groaned and sat up.

Someone had laid a clean dress out over the chair – blue and white, like her own dress. They'd found her some sort of underwear too. She tsked over the antique corset and left it. No idea how to fasten that without help. She lifted the huge bloomers and also decided not to wear them due to a sudden allergy to being drowned in cloth. Her panties, however, were in distinct need of washing. Underwearless for the day then? Did it matter since the hem of the dress went so far south? No.

When she ambled down the internal stairs wearing her new dress, she realized she had no money. Or nothing useful as money in 1860.

Luckily, or unluckily, someone had paid for her room and breakfast.

Madame Betty ushered her to a table near the bar. "Mr. John Beastwood has kindly donated some funds, dear. You go right ahead and eat what you like. You may need the energy later."

Her wink was so suggestive, Virginia had a moment of anxiety – torn between avoiding Mr. Beastwood in case he demanded repayment of the sexual kind, and heading straight for his front door to ask if he wanted it in installments.

Sex with six guns. Her new description for uber alpha male.

Be good. The man was not for her. She had her mission, as the skateboard said. Once upstairs again, she propped it on the chair next to her bed.

"So. Where do I find this power source or the cure?" And how did it know to bring her here, to 1860, to find the cure?

I'm more than a mere skateboard.

sniff

The fuel I need is somewhere underneath Mr. Beastwood's house. The cure is somewhere in this town. The two things are somehow linked.

"Great." She sat back. "Now what do I do? Going near Mr. Beastwood is not safe."

Bleep.

Reconnoiter.

Go look. By checking out his house we may find a solution.

There seemed something terribly wrong about obeying the suggestions of a skateboard. As if she was setting back feminism by a hundred years. Perhaps though, it was a female skateboard?

"From now on, I'll call you Marsha." Fixed that problem.

For a full minute, rude words ran across the board's surface. Most of then began with *F*.

"Wow. Bad board." And why had she thought a skateboard couldn't swear? "You're definitely a Marsha."

On the ground floor, the sides and back of Mr. Beastwood's house were blank. No doors, no windows. Second floor had a balcony, as well as windows and doors, but she couldn't get up there without looking like a burglar.

"What should I do?"

The skateboard was silent. Not a single red pixel crossed its surface.

"What then? Rodney? You want to be called that? Hernandez? Bill?"

Nothing happened.

Crap. It was sulking.

The front of the house was all that was left.

Her first stroll past yielded little due to her speed. To get herself to slow down, she paused to sniff a flower, and then to gently pick a single...red...blossom.

Awestruck, she twirled the severed stem between finger and thumb.

So pretty. The scent of the rose intoxicated. The petals were smooth as satin, luxurious as an Egyptian cotton bath towel, and as beautiful as a new set of saucepans on Mother's Day. Okay, maybe not that last one.

A thorn pricked her thumb. A drop of blood welled and cruised down the stem.

"You touched my roses. Bad move."

She gasped.

John Beastwood was standing over her, watching from the bottom step of the porch, dressed in a black frock coat, two feet away in distance and three hundred feet in height. Slight exaggeration there, but almost true.

Dang it, the man loomed well. Why the fuck was she saying *dang it*? Was there something in the water here?

"Come with me."

Broad daylight, people walking the streets, yet he grabbed her around the neck and hauled her with him into the house. With his other hand over her mouth, she hadn't a chance to scream.

When the door slammed shut at the kick of his boot, he released her mouth. She dropped the skateboard to wrestle more effectively.

After it bounced and clattered to the floor, the skateboard let out a string of bleeps that even sounded like curses. John stared at it then at her, when she sucked in a breath

"Don't bother screaming. It won't reach the outside. Besides, everyone knows the penalty if they touch my flowers. The sheriff told you."

They did? He did? Taunting John Beastwood seemed a good, if perilous, idea. "You make them join your gardening club?"

He pushed her against the wallpapered hallway wall, with his grip still about her throat then curled her hair into a ringlet around his finger. "They're always women. Always, and I keep them with me, in this house, forever."

"Ah." A chill crept up from her ankles, and it wasn't the air conditioning...because there wasn't any. Serial killer alert. "Honestly? I prefer the gardening club."

"I'm sure you would. That position is filled. All I have open is one for an innocent virginal victim who'd like to be ravished endlessly by yours truly, the exceptionally rich, deranged, and angry, John Beastwood."

She pursed her lips and slowly rocked her head back and forth as much as she could while being partly strangled. "Seee. No. Just no. Not my thing. I'm previously engaged, not exactly a virgin, and certainly not innocent."

"What?"

The smile she adopted was hopeful. "Truth."

"My flowers never lie." He lowered his head and growled, gripped her breast, then licked her from cleavage to neck. "You taste like a virgin."

What self-respecting man growled? The licking she'd give a one-off pass to, and maybe the breast clutching. Oh hell, the growling was good too.

"Hey. Hey. Careful with the merchandise."

But as she spoke, he was stripping away her dress. Ripping it at the shoulders, rolling it down then letting it fall. Damn. Caught without underwear, again. This was so familiar.

She was bringing spare panties next time. Ten pair.

"Where is this lover who has already taken your virtue? Where is he?" He forced her up the wall and held her there, her feet dangling, while he perused her naked form.

"You *are* exquisite." He made her open her mouth. "Nice teeth. I look forward to ramming myself into every single one of your holes."

"Dude. Your foreplay sucks."

"You look like a virgin. You taste like one. Where is this so-called lover?"

Whoa, those eyes were getting redder. Her ophthalmologist would have a field day with this guy.

Plucking at her throat, but finding no give in his fingers, she decided she had to tell him something.

"He's in your future, over a hundred years." She thought through that. "Technically, if you stretched the definition, I guess —"

"You're still a virgin." His smile spread. "I believe you. Stranger things have happened. You were meant to come here."

Now that she would have disputed, at length.

"I need to show you my house."

"You do? I could take a rain check? Next Thursday at nine?"

"Now is infinitely better."

The tour through his mansion was fast and furious.

"Smoking room. Dining. Linen closet. Dining. Bathroom. New claw feet on the bath tub. Custom made by the blacksmith."

She peered. All curvy and snaky sculpted steel and...did they have suckers? He dragged her onward. There was little that was decorative or frivolous, only a few potted plants and a few portraits of the same young woman, with blonde hair in a neat pony tail or bun. In every picture, she seemed to be the same age, and it made her wonder if she'd died. How sad.

"Bedroom. Kitchen — that's Rosarita cooking her famous rattlesnake and apple broth. A dose, once a week, keeps my hair sooo glossy." He fluffed his locks with one hand.

"Seriously?" Her abductor was vain, but he did have great hair.

"Hi, Rosarita! I'd love the recipe!" She widened her eyes then whispered rather loudly, "PS. Call the sheriff for me?"

The older woman grinned, her smile pushing out her plump cheeks. She waved her spoon. "Sure, I give you recipe. Have fun, jovencita."

Clearly, not much help there.

John whisked her past the doorway. His recital and house tour went on.

How many dining rooms did you need? Though, crapola, he had truckloads of plates, saucers, candlesticks, and golden knives and forks spilling over the tables in those dining rooms.

"Stairs to the underground cave and lake..."

Down the stairs they went.

"Wait!" Her pleas fell on deaf ears.

Well, not actually deaf. The man *could* hear, but he was too busy dragging her by her hand, and her hair, and carrying her over his shoulder. Naked, over his shoulder. Each jolt as he took a step only emphasized her helplessness and made her pussy get all excited and run about cheering, figuratively speaking.

If it did that for real, she'd need surgery.

God, she ached.

The situation was getting to her. What girl didn't fantasize about being dragged away over a man's shoulder to his underground lair? Granted, she'd done this before but the allure never went away.

They reached the underground cavern – stalagmites, stalactites, and a glowing blue lake not far away.

"For your first time, this will do." By her neck, he pinned her against a thick timber pole.

Damn convenient pole. Always, the neck. Think of how much easier it would be to escape if she was minus a neck. Then he proceeded to get naked too. One handed – so dexterous.

His many leather gun belts were unbuckled and lowered, other belts were undone. He used one to fasten her hands behind the pole and a second to tie her neck to it.

Black leather boots were kicked off, pants were removed, shirts unbuttoned and thrown aside.

Leather, leather, leather, leather!

Mmm. Knew it! Leather underpants.

If only she was certain she wasn't going to be buried somewhere afterward, she'd have been happier.

Then, *ohmigod*, the piece de resistance. From behind his back, his tentacles unfurled, ebony ones that glistened, with cute little suckers.

His color scheme was so predictable. If the man used nail polish, it'd be black. Deep skin cleanser facial mask – black. Post-it notes – black.

Nevertheless.

"Tentacles!" she shrieked joyfully, jiggling a little against the pole. That, gave him pause.

"What? I scared you? Good." He glowered, flexing tentacles, making them curl, uncurl, and wave about above her head.

Virginia sucked her lip into her mouth and nibbled. She hated spoiling people's little parties.

Did she have to pop his bubble? Really?

"You did scare me! You did. Oh, the horror. Tentacles are my worst –"

"I can tell that you're lying." With ominous languor, several of his tentacles wrapped around and around her, caressing her body, playing. His voice dropped to that bottom of the ocean sound, like gravel shifting on sand. With her ear tickling from his breath, she considered fainting.

"When I take you, Miss Virginia..." More heavy breathing.

Gawwwd. Said like that, with him almost inhaling her ear, even her own name sounded like sex.

"When I invade your body, when I possess you, it will be your first *something*. That is my signature." He nodded, eyes narrowing, one tentacle tip sliding between her legs, slippery and succulent, back and forth, up and down.

She moved her legs apart, just a little. Wouldn't do to appear too wanton.

My, my, myyy. Her brain shut down, momentarily. "Mmm. Oh. Nngahhh." *Left a half inch.*

"Nnngah? Am I getting you aroused? Wet? You feel *very* wet."

"Swahili, that was Swahili for..."

Her inner voice mumbled, *you're a dick?*

You are so dead. "For, have a nice day?"

"Liar. Such a cute liar. But, I can work with this. Tell me, my dear girl, what haven't you done that excites you?"

"Ah. Oh. Let's see. This may take a while." She should lie, out of loyalty to Karl. Could John really tell if she lied? She could start with the weird ones. Maybe he'd get bored?

Only took twelve suggestions before he let her go and fetched coffee, whisky, two chairs, a quill, and some writing paper.

"Now. Astronaut sex? Is that a real thing?" His voice rose in puzzlement. He licked the quill and poised it above the paper.

CHAPTER 6

He sat still for writing down twenty-two of her suggested weirdest of the weird fetishes that he couldn't possibly do. Then he cracked.

Who'd have thought the man would be ingenious enough to fetch the skateboard and interrogate it? After he held it above the lake and threatened to drop it into the deep, phosphorescent water, the thing spilled the beans.

Listening to it cough up all her fetishes, she realized that, dammit, the thing *could* read her mind.

"Lies, all lies. You'd believe a futuristic device over *moi?*" Though she squeaked in surprise, he pulled her off the chair she sat on and dragged her to his discarded clothes.

"Leather fetish *and* you've never fucked a cowboy or done it in a lake?"

Face to face, John hugged her closer. He'd tucked away his tentacles while they'd talked, but his erection pulsed against her stomach.

"The cowboy part is easy."

Grinning triumphantly, he lifted her off her feet then slid his cock along between her legs, pushing aside her lower lips like a steamship parting waves – a ten inch steamship in the shape of a schlong that no doubt carried a full crew of eager seamen...and if this simile got any crazier she'd be forced to kill the author with a fork.

"Woman, I'm always a cowboy."

This was getting a little too serious for a first date.

"Never an Indian?"

He chuckled. "Never."

Then he came in for a kiss, slow and with maximum eye contact, like if he looked away she might vamoose. By the time his lips met hers, she was going cross-eyed.

She might be his prisoner, but she really shouldn't be co-operating in her own ravishment, should she? She attempted to duck aside.

"Uh-uh." His hand at her nape squeezed in and held her still.

"Heyyy. No fair."

"I never, ever, play fair."

With his cock surging back and forth in the groove made by her pussy, and his mouth intent on conquering hers by crushing her lips and doing war with her tongue, her concentration went bye byes.

Her eyes rolled up and, *damn*, she was already cross-eyed. *Ow, my eyeballs.*

Simply feeling what he did to her became her universe.

Even an angel couldn't resist this primitive appeal to her dirty, depraved, animalistic subconscious. Her bad, naughty, evil subconscious.

Are you getting this skateboard? Store it away in your memory.

Karl would surely understand the attraction of Mr. Beastwood to her animal *id*, seeing he was himself part octopus creature from another dimension.

Slip. Slide. And a thrust that nearly breached her inner sanctum. All that was needed was another quarter of an inch. If she wiggled, mightn't he enter her? She tried hard, straining to make him do it, puffing at her exertions. But no, he tightened his arms, his biceps solid barriers to her going anywhere he didn't want her to go.

"Your favorite little fantasies and fetishes? I can do them all," he said hoarsely.

"You can?" Virginia sighed and wiggled her butt. That last thrust – such a tease this man was.

"I can. Even the upside-down-like-a-bat one. But not the astronaut." He sank his teeth into her shoulder, making her squeal, sending liquid pleasure rippling through her. "I think this may take a while."

Yes, please.

His magnificent tentacles emerged again, to wrap her at waist or arms or neck, as necessary, holding her in place while he bound her in leather at wrists, ankles, and elbows, and that was just for starters.

Buckles were buckled. Tongues of metal slipped into their holes in the leather. As those tiny holes were violated, Beastwood played with hers – her nether hole and her pussy entrance, her mouth, even her ears, toying with them delicately, roughly, rawly. Lots and lots of *ly* words barged in and demanded some screentime.

Passionately rudely elbowed the others aside. The queen of vaudeville adverbs had arrived.

Passion, panting, and penises – it was one of Virginia's last coherent thoughts. After that she was lucky to remember her birthday.

He made her want, ache, throb, and plead. All manner of unladylike sounds emerged from her mouth.

"Fff... No, mmm, oh. Fuck yes!"

While he wrenched in the leather, he teased her nipples, drawing them out with the suckers on his tentacles. He made it impossible for her to move and difficult for her to breathe, unless he wanted her to, and yet he cinched the leather in another fraction. Tight.

Tighter.

The smell intoxicated her. The grip of the belts and his tentacles both subdued her and aroused her.

Raising her a few feet above the ground and away from his body, he examined her, clicking his tongue. His great tentacles suspended her with ease, barely swaying.

"Such a work of art, my pretty. All you need is my care and attention. I have you, Virginia. I am a were-squid and you are my prey, to be teased and taunted, to be ravaged, penetrated, and defiled, at my pleasure."

Just his words made her moisten and she squirmed as if trying to get free, though truthfully she only tested his bonds. *Caught. Oh, yes.*

"You cannot escape."

As if she would, now. The man had no clue. Once more, a tentacle wormed between her legs, so wonderfully squirmy and wet when it bathed in what dripped from her. She sighed, close to begging for more in-depth attention.

Fuck me, Sir.

"What have I found? A well of feminine nectar? A pulsating delight of hidden treasure?"

A what? No, she thought, startled at his effervescent euphemisms that made her think of Victorian ladies skipping through greenhouses watering their plants. *No, it's my cunt.*

Though the space was tight because of her ankles being tied, he forced his way along until the tip curled out to dawdle in her ass crack. Then he spun her so she faced away and looked down at an angle at the floor. With a tentacle wrapped about her legs, he forced her to bend at the waist.

She gasped, suspecting where this was headed. One of Karl's favorites but not always hers. Surely they hadn't discovered anal sex in 1860! *Quelle horreur!*

"Not there!"

"No?" Beastwood chuckled and rearranged her, spreading her thighs apart a few more inches. "Not where? I was only checking you were well-lubricated, but you have me curious. Was it here, you referred to? Hmm?"

"Eeek!" A tentacle tip probed her anally, sinking in slowly, ever so slowly, turning like a screw as it did so.

"Or was it here, you meant?"

A second tentacle squeezed between her pussy lips, relentless as the tide. Both tentacles forged onward, tunneling, worming. She could hear the muted squelch, feel the coolness on her inner thighs of her own juices. Again, she strained at the leather binding her elbows and wrists, and there was no give.

"Not. There. Please?"

For an exquisite few moments, moments that that had her arching her spine, *more, oh god, more,* he thrust in and out, going further, until it seemed something the size of a baseball bat was inside her.

Which, from memory, was pretty accurate. She hurriedly decided that, for once, her memory must be wrong. Tennis racquet size? But which end? Oh fuckit. Whatever. Who cared?

The next few thrusts hit somewhere *gooood.*

She lowered her head, her mouth gaping and drooling, her moans quiet and desperate. This both hurt and sent her soaring with pleasure.

So full. Her heart pumped lust into her lower body, engorging her lips, making her clit seem ready to erupt – and this time she zoomed past the visual. No exploding clits. With every single beat of heart and push of tentacle, she ascended toward climax.

The belts, above and below her breasts, made them bulge. Her nipples, that were normally such shy and sulky things, become as prominent as the cherries on a sundae.

Two spare tentacles wound their way to her breasts, wrapping them in a crushing spiral until her breasts protruded even more. She looked down, to see the very tips of those tentacles settle across her nipples in a gentle helix of tiny suction cups. They stroked at her and sucked.

Her swear words became incomprehensible and possibly Swahili.

"Shhh. None of that." Then he stuffed a last writhing tentacle down her throat at the same time as the ones inside her other holes withdrew then rammed into her.

She couldn't breathe, couldn't talk, couldn't do anything but be obliterated by a stupendous orgasm that wrung her dry of sanity.

Her screams were muffled. Her shudders and writhing, and the bowing of her spine, took her precisely nowhere except launching into...

Ecstasy.

The nowhere land of pleasure.

When she surfaced, she was in the lake with him, curled in his lap, cradled by water, his arms, and his kisses. Her bottom stung like Hell.

"Most beautiful woman, you tempt me so thoroughly."

"Mmm." Nice man. Sexy were-squid man.

"Fetish one and two down. Only eighteen to go."

She summoned up a gargled, "Nnng?" from the depths of her sore throat, then a disbelieving arch of brow. The words *later*, or *tomorrow*, or *not yet*, all occurred to her but none would escape from her lips. She'd even lost the *ah* from her *nnngah*.

Her mind was a little gone. Beastwood had exploded it like the Deathstar had the planet Alderan. She'd have to collect the bits in a jar and glue them back in. That bad.

"You may thank me later. Upside down like a bat? Oh. Wait."

Something nudged her foot. In the glowing blue water, a creature swam, long and sinuous, and at times sparkly.

"You mentioned electrical play? I've heard of this new invention by Edison called electricity. I believe he has linked these eels to it."

Eels? Her eyes bulged so much that she was sure that, in another second, they'd plop into the water...where these electrical eels would eat them. Her eyes were having a bad day, overall.

"Let's do some upside-down electrical play."

With eels?

Noooooooooo.

She ran out of *O*'s for her *no* before John Beastwood had her slung upside down. Slowly he lowered her into the water, headfirst.

An eel swam past.

She burbled out curses, watched the bubbles of air waft upward, heard his muffled reply through the water. "We can do three fetishes! Breath control. Count to fifteen."

Oh, man. She was going to kill him several times over, if she survived. Then he stuffed the first tentacle into her pussy, and managed to find her mouth with his cock. Her favorite lollipop.

Automatically, already halfway to wonderland, she licked him and let him slide to the back of her throat. Something nudged her clit and started to play with it like a conductor performing his best ever kinky concerto. *Suck. Suck. Squeeze.*

She writhed and managed to raise her head from the water and gasp in some air.

John let her do so, then lowered her back in.

Ugh. There was some odd appeal to such possession. Killing him could wait.

The first eel zapped her breast.

No, killing was good.

And p-p-plug his dick into a light socket, suggested her alarmed inner voice.

For once, they agreed.

They reached fourteen fetishes before John Beastwood called it a day. "You are so naughty. This century, and me, just grew grey hairs."

She purred, her eyelids at half-mast, while stroking the tentacle that had flopped over her belly. The furs they lay on were super comfy and she was exhausted.

"Poor man. I mean poor were-squid. For the best though. My lover, Karl Thulhu should have me for the last fetishes."

He raised himself on his elbow, scowling down at her. "You can never return to him."

Ah. Problem.

CHAPTER 7

"Why?" Her question was earnest and it gave him pause, made him sit back. Had no one ever questioned him?

"It is how it is. My captives stay with me."

"Until what?" She had to find out. "How many women have you abducted and ravished?"

His steady regard gave little away. "Too many to count without an abacus."

She couldn't ask this with him staring down at her and she too levered herself onto her elbow. If this provoked some rage, so be it. John Beastwood did seem unhinged even if he was an expert lover. "How many have you killed?"

His answer took a long time to emerge. "None."

That was it?

"Is there a fast way to get you to tell me all this without asking a thousand questions?"

"No."

She drummed her fingers. "I need to go back to my time, to Karl."

"You will stay with me until you do what all of my victims do. You will transmute into gold."

"Gold?"

Yup. Unhinged. Where were all the golden statues of women? There were none so he was lying. *He probably ate them.*

Now wasn't that a cheerful thought? How to ask that without being too obvious?

The skateboard had ended up a few feet away and she rolled it to her with her toe.

Running across the surface was a revelation. It'd found the power source. The lake water.

She could return to Karl, given five minutes alone with this thing. Return uneaten, hopefully.

"So..." With her forefinger, she rocked the skateboard back and forth on the fur. "What do you suppose human flesh tastes like?"

John groaned and collapsed onto his back. "I didn't eat them!"

"No? Then what?"

"I think you are both the smartest woman I've met and the dumbest. I am constantly amazed at how you go from one extreme to the other."

If you haven't got anything smart to say, don't say anything at all? Nah.

"Let me guess. You...skinned them and used the skin to paper the walls? Or, or," She jerked, excited. "Are they *in* the walls? Wait, no, I haven't heard any moaning. What else? The rattlesnake broth is really them?"

"Nooo." He covered his face with his splayed fingers. "Stop! I'll tell you, just no more scary stories."

"Oh. Okay."

"They turned into the gold tableware and candlesticks you saw in the dining rooms and at night they come out and sing and dance."

What. The. Fuck.

"I think..." Virginia wobbled her head, deciding. "I think I prefer you papering your walls with skin." She glared. "No one turns into a fork!"

"Suit yourself."

Late that night, he set up chairs in the biggest dining room. As a treat, Rosarita brought them both goblets of white wine, roast chicken, and bowls of rattlesnake and apple broth.

"Yum-mee." She plastered on a smile.

Rosarita slipped a piece of paper into her hand. "Here's the recipe. Don't burn your tongue. It's hot." For a woman, she had hairy hands.

At the stroke of midnight, Virginia nearly swallowed her tongue.

"Wow! Who'd have thought?"

"I know," he said sadly. "I know. First time it happened, in 1829, I thought I'd found a great way to make money. I sold a few but I've got far more gold in veins in the cavern." He shook his head. "I'm tired of my compulsion to take a new victim. The townsfolk send for mail order brides. A month or two and she's gone, like the others. Like all the others..."

There was a precedent for this. People mutating into cutlery? She'd heard of it happening once before. Mr. Beastwood and his beauties were not unique. Be damned, if she could recall when or how.

The tableware began a new routine, lining up on the table's edge and kicking up their tines and serrated blades like can-can dancers.

"Pity the candlestick's off key."

"Mmm."

The skateboard bleeped. She leaned over to read.

"Uh-huh. Uh-huh. Hmm. Right. I see."

Then she leaned back to him and whispered in his ear, "Have none of the women ever escaped?"

"You're still hoping?" The deep breath he took made her wonder if he was as devoid of humanity as this insane, domineering, tyrannical were-squid seemed to be, on the surface. "One, I let go."

"Why?"

"I loved her. I didn't want to have to see her turn into a fork." John blew his nose on a corner of the tablecloth. "Or a knife."

"Why hasn't Rosarita changed? Because you don't screw her?"

"She's a werewolf. I think she's got enough weird anatomy. She seems immune."

Werewolves *and* transmutating women?

"And men never change?"

"I don't employ them. Only Rafe, for a few months to help with repairs. The sheriff too. He did some odd jobs for me as a teenager. Kept him out of trouble."

"John, what if I could solve your problem? I can show you how to stop them changing."

"You expect me to believe that you, a woman only recently arrived in my house, has figured this out when I could not over thirty years!"

"My skateboard figured it out."

He nodded. "That, I can see."

Chauvinistic bastard.

"How? Tell me and you may go free. Wait, it's pointless even so."

"Why?" Mere inches away from freedom. Why did he baulk? "You can have companionship, a lifelong partner, someone who loves you, not just a short-term victim cross lover. Why not?"

He shook his head.

Oh. Oh no. Some tragedy was hidden here. "Is she passed on? Dead? Living in another country?" His expression only grew sadder, longer, like a big unhappy puppy dog, one with six tentacles. "Or, oh dear, does she not love you back?"

John winced. "No, she does not." He wiped his palm over his face. "I destroyed what we had. I drove her away. Told her I was no good for her. She lives near here, pretends to be a widow. I gifted her a farm, but she'd never have me back."

She regarded him. Perhaps he was correct? After all, who could a billionaire were-squid gunslinger ever be good for except someone with a thing for rich boyfriends, calamari, and violence?

Wait. She thought for a second. *That's me.*

But she was weird.

It never hurt to try.

Virginia turned on her chair to face him fully. "We are going to try. Minuses. You are a bit of an asshole. Ninety nine percent asshole on my asshole meter. But I can teach you, remake you, give you social graces. I will rebuild you into the ultimate rich, if a little ruthless – since women love that shit – sexy bastard, with a smidge of asshole."

"I..." He cocked a brow. "Am an asshole?"

She sat up properly. "Yes. You shove your tentacles halfway down a woman's throat on your first date."

"Minor."

"Also." She counted on her fingers. "Do tentacle anal without asking. Drown them. Zap them."

"You listed those. Most. I just did them."

"Only because you asked. I didn't say go ahead! You can't do that, not if you want to keep her."

"I could just tie her up for eternity and lock the damn doors."

"*Tsk,* John. No. Trust me. Just no. Not if you love her."

His irises cycled through every flaring, fiery color on the color wheel – demonic red, passionate orange, kill-them-all violet, before setting for black. "I suppose. I see. I will change this."

"You don't give women any say in what happens to them."

"They're women." He shrugged.

She resisted knifing him with a...she searched about...skateboard. Luckily, her PMS had slithered away for a month.

"I open doors for them too." He looked upwards for a second. "The ones that don't lead outside."

"You abduct all your women against their will."

"Mmm." John sniffed. "I told you, I'm going to give that one up."

"All of them. You have to give all of them up, if you want this woman to return to your arms."

The way he stared at the floor was new. "To get Abby back in my arms, I would do anything."

"Good. Now. I need paper, ink, and that quill."

"For?" But he stood, shoving back his chair.

"Writing my book – Social Etiquette for Gunslinger Were-squids."

"One last thing before we begin. Why do the women change? Aren't you worried about yourself?"

Should she reveal this? What if he took this secret and still kept her locked up? She had to, surely? She had to trust him at some point.

Virginia stood. "It's the lake. The water. Perhaps only by bathing in it, but I noticed even your drinking water is tinted a slight blue."

He staggered. "The water in the lake? Is this certain? I'd never have let this happen."

"Ninety-seven percent certain according to The Gospel of the Skateboard. What I don't understand is why the rest of the women in the town aren't affected."

"The rocks keep the water out of the town's supply. If only I'd known about this!"

The stricken look on his face said he was genuinely sorry, but she kept her sympathy to a minimum. He hadn't said he wouldn't have abducted and ravished those women, just that he wouldn't have let them drink the water. If she could get this woman to love him, Peckerwood Springs would be a far safer place.

"Can I ask you something personal, John?"

"Yes. Though I may not answer it."

"Were you always a were-squid? Was your father one?"

His gaze locked onto hers, as if searching out her frailties, and he seemed to look deep down into the very depths of her soul where no one else had ever been – except for her inner voice when she was looking for hot chocolate in the middle of the night. She was not without flaws, she knew this.

"Virginia, you've got a spot of chicken there." He tapped his chin. "But, your question. I was not born this way. My father was not one. He was never here. I am the man who built this place. I may even be immortal." He shrugged. "If so, I've saved a lot of rent over the years. I changed when I was twenty-one. Over the course of several months, I grew my tentacles, and at the same time, I discovered my insatiable desire for women and the pleasures of the flesh."

"Thank you for answering. The tentacles – unfortunate. The pleasures of the flesh – normal for a man."

"It is?" His eyebrows sprang up.

"Yup. It's the kidnapping that's wrong."

"Ohhh."

She had so much to teach this man...squid...gunslinger...asshole.

CHAPTER 8

For a whole week, they concentrated on his jogging, weight-lifting, and sparring.

After the tenth sprint up the stairs that morning, John came to a stop, resting his hands on his knees while he recovered.

"Why are we doing this? I thought it'd be more kissing and dancing?"

"Ah. You're right. Fuck. That was Rocky!" She blamed the music running through her head. He would've been a good contender for world heavyweight too.

"If you were mine, I'd wash out your little mouth for that curse word."

"Mmm." Wide-eyed, and a little aroused at his dominance, she backed a step and made a note not to take out all the asshole. It was cute.

They began.

Dancing. Choosing clothes. First date kisses – interesting to practice. Door opening. Spreading one's cloak over puddles. No anal until the third date.

Getting there. Slowly. Tediously, except for when he accidentally ravished her, once or twice. The man was learning.

By the end of the week, she had him opening the main house door for her, even if he did grit his teeth and have a muscle spasm stopping himself from grabbing her neck.

"Good boy!" Virginia beamed and stuck the gold star to his coat. Then she skipped away fast.

His foot got in the way and she would've face planted on the floor, but he caught her at the last second.

177

"There's only so much I can take. *Good boy* is not one of them."

Then he sat on a chair, bent her over his lap, flipped up her dress, and spanked her hard. It was a lovely diversion for them both. The week had been hard and grueling and filled with only three sex scenes that for some strange reason the author didn't detail. Probably because they were boring average tentacle sex.

And because John was supposed to be devoted to Abby by now.

"Shame on you, John." She rubbed her warmed up bottom, smiling at the welts from his fingers. "No more sex."

He sighed, shrugged. "I apologize. I didn't not write them."

True.

The man had apologized! This was progress.

There was a barn dance in a week. He would be ready by then.

She cranked up the gruellingness a few notches. More dancing, more kissing and holding doors, less...she meant NO anal, or sex, at all. None.

Goddammit, he was gorgeous when he was mean. In seven days she had his asshole percentage down to fourteen percent, twenty-two on a bad day. Perfection.

They rode to the barn dance on his stallion, Big Donger. She had a feeling the horse had been drinking too much blue water. She rode at the front, side saddle. Her inner city girl existence in the twenty-first century had not exposed her to horse riding. Nor had it exposed her to being felt up by tentacles while on a horse.

"John!" She turned in the saddle to glare. "Have you not learned? We are going to meet your...your previous victim, your Abby."

His eyes were as steady as a train going up a steep incline with Indians bearing down on it and about to blow up the track. Plus the passengers were screaming.

She tensed, waiting for his argument.

"I truly must be monogamous?"

"Yes."

"Crap." But he flicked the reins and they trotted onward.

The barn doors were open and the lanterns showed a mess of dancers already strutting their stuff. Violins, fiddles, banjos, and someone had brought a harmonica. It was bedlam and so much fun.

A few cows and chickens wandered in and out at their leisure, perhaps enjoying the music.

Within a second of them walking in through the doors, he saw

Abby. She *was* the woman in the portraits. Though Virginia hadn't asked him, it was her. Pretty, maybe prettier. Perhaps ten years older than she'd been in the painting.

How many years had he pined for her?

John knew she hadn't married. As he strode to Abby, her smile blossomed. All these years she'd waited for him to return.

The man had a chance.

The training paid off – not a step did he put wrong in the dancing or the social chat or in the simply being attentive and loving, apart from that one time he grabbed her and bent her backward, against the hay bale, for a tongue kiss. Abby seemed to like it, so Virginia gave him a pass.

As the band began to play what would be the last jig of the night, John came to her.

"You have worked miracles," he whispered. "She still wants to be mine. I'm going to ask her to marry me."

"Now? Tonight?"

"Yes." No hesitation. "She will agree. I know this."

Oh my. Rejection would not sit well with this man. She crossed her fingers as the dance began and he took Abby in his arms and whirled her away.

At the end, when the banjo plunked out the last note, people seemed to realize what was happening. They cleared a space for the couple. John had gone to one knee before her.

Aww. Virginia wiped at her eyes. *Sweet.*

Everyone watched and listened, as he said those magical words, "Will you marry me?"

They all sighed together and cheered when she softly answered, "Yes," with a smile big enough to light up the barn.

Then Virginia watched in horror when the back of his shirt ripped and he swept Abby into the air with his tentacles. No one spoke. No cloth rustled. No one coughed or sneezed. The barn had fallen silent. Slowly John lowered Abby and placed her behind him.

She hadn't been certain, but it was clear that he'd never, in all the past decades, shown his were-squidliness to these people in full light.

This could be bad.

"What are you looking at, my friends?" He nudged back his coat, but on this night he wore no gun.

"You're a monster!" a girl shrieked. That released them. A storm of voices erupted, screaming, shouting, accusing. When they surged forward, there was death on their faces.

"Kill him!"

He and Virginia made it to the horse ahead of the mob and galloped back to his mansion with men riding after them.

She half-turned so he could hear her. "You're going to have to run from here! Leave Peckerwood!"

"Never!" His growl was so beastlike, she shivered. This night would not end well.

"You cannot, must not, kill them all."

He was silent.

She would never forget how Abby's fingers had slipped from his or the look on her face of terror and loss, of ultimate loss. Her scream of "Johnnnn," and her sobs, echoed in Virginia's mind.

It was almost as bad as losing car keys down a storm drain.

Wait, this is a love story now, sort of. That simile was so embarrassingly impersonal and rude.

Almost as bad as losing your cat down a storm drain?

Okay, stopping there.

Unrequited love is not funny.

It's tragic.

Must. Not. Make. Joke.

No bunnies in blenders.

Noooo! Don't take my keyboard!

After several months of therapy, the author had her keyboard returned to her.

Desperate jokes require desperate measures.

CHAPTER 9

When they reached the main street and were galloping toward his mansion, Virginia was stunned to see several of Karl's biker gang lined up before it.

"The Sea Wolves are here?"

"Who are they?" John almost snarled. A mite upset?

"Karl's men. They can help us. If they're here, they must have a portal. We can take you back to our time."

Souleater, Dangerous Bob, Heart Surgeon, and Horse, the man she'd once embarrassed by referring to his small schlong size. She'd almost regretted that until he tried to dry hump her at the edge of a cliff.

Saved. She didn't want a battle. This could so easily become a slaughter.

Their pursuers had arrived – most of the townsmen. Somehow, they'd grabbed pitchforks and torches along the way and the sky above them was wreathed in flame and poked by the little pointy ends of the pitchforks.

"Always the pitchforks," John muttered. "How easily they have turned on me. Virginia, I will not yield to these men. I will not turn tail and flee to your time. If I cannot be with Abby, so be it. I would

181

rather die here."

As they drew nearer, their ugly curses became clearer.

John strode to the front. "Why must you persecute me? Have I not saved you from being killed, molested, and robbed by bandits a hundred times over?"

A bearded man stepped forward, torch and pistol in his hands. "You have revealed yourself to be a monster. A foul being with big long slimy tentacle things. How can we ever allow you, you creature from the depths of the ocean, or from Hell itself, to stay in our town. Go! Before we must kill you. Go. Let us burn your hell nest." He gestured with the torch at the mansion.

Dangerous Bob came up beside Virginia, the skateboard tucked under his arm. His usual articulate swearing translated instantly. "Fuckitty fuck grr? Fuckerr." *Want us to do something, Miss? Karl sent us to fetch you after the skateboard came home.*

"It did?" Her voice rose to a squeak. "What about the cure for Karl?"

"Fuckiter Frr. Grr fuck." *We have it. The recipe given to you was it. The skateboard came with us to show the way. You can either come through the portal with us, or use the skateboard to return.*

"Neither. I have to help John." Unrequited love. How could she refuse?"

They want to kill him because he's got tentacles?

"Yes."

So. We kill the people?

"No! No damn killing!"

"Fuckerr." Which meant plain ol' fuck.

Beyond Dangerous Bob, the massive and menacing Souleater grumbled. Though he seemed merely a big man, like most of the Sea Wolves he had another form. His flesh flickered and blurred in places – signs of him barely restraining himself from transforming into a shark. Here, in a desert? More bad things.

She sighed.

While they'd talked, the townsfolk had crept a few steps closer. The glaring and swearing match seemed ready to come to a boil. What could she do? They hated him. Despised him. Yet he wanted to stay and marry Abby.

In times of stress, she went into automatic mode. Her instinctive schlong detector assessed each man who faced them. She noted some oddities. The sheriff was a ten incher. She'd missed that in the dark, the other night. Even Rafe was here. Traitors, or just scared men? After all the people he'd shot for them. So ungrateful.

Their spokesman launched into another tirade. "We will never allow you to exist here. Go back to your crack in the ground. Begone! Your foul stench invades my nostrils and turns my stomach."

John growled, again, flexed his hands over his nonexistent gun belt. At the back of the crowd, a rider galloped up and hauled their mount to a dusty halt. Abby.

Oh god. What she might witness.

On the far right fringe of the crowd, a man let out a scream and rushed forward brandishing a saber and a torch. "Yaaaaaaaa!"

To Virginia's appalled surprise, John stood there, chest out, defenseless. The saber rose and she winced, expecting his death as it plunged into his chest. Instead Souleater snapped into his seven foot tall, four foot wide shark form, opened his many-toothed mouth wide, and swallowed the man whole. The saber rattled to the ground. Smoke puffed from Souleater's mouth and he spat out the torch...a few seconds later, he burped. Then he flash-changed back into man form.

Stunned silence.

"Neat," said John.

"Fuck," added Dangerous Bob.

"Heyyy," said the spokesperson, futilely waving his pistol. "What? What..."

Oh boy.

Delayed schlong stats swarmed her brain. The sheriff, Rafe, a random dude. All ten inchers when extrapolated to fully erect form.

"Ohmigod!" she gasped. *Yes, oh yes. Of course.*

"Where'd he go?" asked the spokesman.

She had to act while they were still stunned. *Carpe diem* thingo. Seize the day of the cock and all that.

"John." She tugged on his coat. "I can fix this, I think. You said the sheriff and Rafe worked for you. What about that man?" She singled out random dude.

183

"Yes, he did. Only a short time. Why? How can that solve this? I'm tired of hiding. If they don't want me here..."

"No. Wait." She stepped to the front and waved her arms above her head. "I have a solution!"

The spokesman scratched his beard with the bad end of the pistol. Her eye twitched and she prayed it wouldn't fire.

"What is it? Can you drop this terrible fiend, this anathema, this monster of monsters, into a pit of burning lava?"

"Um, no." *Bloodthirsty fuckers.* "What is the one thing you most desire in life? Because John can give it to you."

That got them thinking. Most of them joined in and threw out answers. "Good plumbing." "Fresh bear on Thursdays." "Women!"

By the end of a short debate, the spokesman, hat in hand, and pistol now pointing at his balls...*yikes*, declared the winning entry, "Happiness. Give us that." He sneered.

The Sea Wolves made angry noises. She had to get this done fast or they'd eat another of the crowd.

"And here is why John can gift you with happiness."

"I can?" John was puzzled.

"Yes," She hissed out the corner of her mouth. "The water. All the men who worked for you have ten inch schlongs. It grows cocks! It's why you have tentacles. You were exposed for years. In small doses..."

"Ahhh. You *are* smart."

"Happiness? Come on. Answer us." The spokesman jeered. The crowd murmured evilly.

She prayed this would do it. "He can give you happiness because..." Dramatic pause. Wait for it. "He can give you cocks the size of donkeys."

Oops. Well, she meant the size of donkey cocks, not the size of a donkey. A cock that big would be a little inconvenient.

No one had noticed. *Phew.*

Dead silence reigned. A whore staggered across in the gap between John and the townsfolk and none of the men moved.

"Fuck," one whispered. "Really?"

"The sheriff, Rafe, and random dude are proof! They *all* have ten inch peckers. You know this, yes?"

The crowd murmured agreement. The spokesman looked around at them.

She had these men, almost, in the palm of her hand, defective peckers and all. "Think how your wives and girlfriends will be amazed. Think of the benefits. What more could you ask for?"

More silence. Then a few "Hell yeahs," perforated the night. The whore wandered through again, singing.

"It's working." John put his hand on her shoulder. "It's working!"

"What about the *throw the monster into the pot of doom* thing?" someone asked.

"It's fine." The spokesman shuffled his feet and stuck a fixed smile on his face. "No hard feelings, hey John? Bygones be bygones."

"None. All I want is to live here peacefully, barring shooting the odd bandit, with Abby as my wife." His hand squeezed on Virginia's shoulder. She swore she could hear tears in his voice.

"But, but, but," someone stuttered. "They ate...him! You know."

"Who?" The spokesman frowned. "Him?"

"Yeah. Him."

"Who was he?" someone else asked.

A suggestion was tossed out. "Cannon fodder?"

"Ohhh," they all sighed. "That. Poor man."

"There you go then." The spokesman turned to the crowd. "A terribly sad but necessary death. Three seconds silence, please. In memoriam of cannon fodder."

Unsure what the hell was happening, Virginia bowed her head for the three seconds.

The spokesman then faced her and John again, grinning. "Done!" He clapped his hands together and waited, shifting from foot to foot. "Can we have them now?"

John swallowed. The prospect of growing cocks seemed to be bothering him.

She nudged him. "You'll be fine."

"Of course." He straightened. "It requires a special medicine. It will take some months, but I will guarantee the results."

"Excellent. We all good with John's promise?"

The roar made the windows of the town shake.

Jeez. Men!

Then Abby arrived, strolling through the crowd, hips swaying, as if parting the red sea. Her smile was back and John gathered her into his side and kissed the top of her head.

"My love. At last we are together."

"Yes, we are, John." She turned up her face and he cradled her chin. Her stray blonde locks, that had escaped from her bun, curled over his fingers.

"You are more beautiful than I remembered."

Watching them kiss seemed an invasion of privacy, but Virginia grinned and watched anyway, along with half the town.

Perhaps he had truly found his perfect partner. She seemed a little innocent. Then she peeked out from within his hug, with one eye. "Psst. Were you his last girl?"

Was she? Virginia guessed so. "Yes."

"Want to join in the fun later? You know, in the lake."

What? She clicked. "Ahhh. No."

"Hmm. Pity." Abby snuggled back into him.

She blinked. What the hell had that been? Definitely, Abby was a good match for this man, this beast man.

Everything was humming along. People were happy, chatting, and totally over the slaughtering each other idea. The wedding would be a cinch – the tableware was already organized.

It was time to leave.

"How is Karl?" Virginia said, in an aside to Dangerous Bob.

Still moaning and clutching his head. All done here?

"Yes." She took one last look at the happy couple and whispered to them, "Goodbye and good luck." Then she sank back into the line of the Sea Wolves.

The skateboard would do. Portals gave her nausea, bad. She took the skateboard from Bob. "Meet you back home." Then she stepped on and gave the command.

"Home."

The world fuzzed into that electric blue and the wind whirled. They were off.

"Rome?" bleeped the skateboard.

Now, it talked?

Rome? Ohhh fuck.

ABOUT CARI SILVERWOOD

Cari Silverwood is a New York Times and USA Today bestselling writer of kinky darkness or sometimes of dark kinkiness (and sometimes spoofs), depending on her moods and the amount of time she's spent staring into the night.

When others are writing bad men doing bad things, you may find her writing good men who accidentally on purpose fall into the abyss and come out with their morals twisted in knots.

If you'd like to learn more or join my mailing list go to www.carisilverwood.net
Also Facebook & Goodreads:
http://www.facebook.com/cari.silverwood
http://www.goodreads.com/author/show/4912047.Cari_Silverwood

You're welcome to join this group on facebook to discuss Cari Silverwood's books:
https://www.facebook.com/groups/864034900283067/

Also by Cari Silverwood

Dark hearts Series
(Dark erotic fiction)
Wicked Ways
Wicked Weapon
Wicked Hunt

Pierced Hearts Series
(Dark erotic fiction)
Take me, Break me
Klaus
Bind and Keep me
Make me Yours Evermore
Seize me From Darkness
Yield

Preyfinders Series
(Erotic scifi)
Precious Sacrifice
Intimidator
Defiler
Preyfinders – The Trilogy
Preyfinders Universe
Cyberella
Squirm Files Series
(Parodies of erotic romance)
Squirm – virgin captive of the billionaire biker tentacle monster
Strum – virgin captive of the billionaire demon rock star monster
The Well-hung Gun – virgin captive of the billionaire were-squid gunslinger monster
The Squirm Files anthology
The Badass Brats Series
The Dom with a Safeword
The Dom on the Naughty List
The Dom with the Perfect Brats
The Dom with the Clever Tongue
The Steamwork Chronicles Series
Iron Dominance
Lust Plague
Steel Dominance
Others
31 Flavors of Kink
Three Days of Dominance
Rough Surrender
Blood Glyphs
Cataclysm Blues (a free erotic post apocalyptic novella)
Needle Rain (epic fantasy – not erotic)
My Romance Curse (romantic comedy)
Fan Anonymous (a spoof of a kinky author biography)
Magience – non-erotic, epic fantasy
Needle Rain – set in the magience world but with erotic scenes

Printed in Great Britain
by Amazon

21671750R00108